TERI WOODS

PRESENTS

DEADLY REIGNS

III

THE THIRD OF A TRILOGY

For information on how individual consumers can place orders, please write to Teri Woods Publishing, P.O. Box 20069, New York, NY 10001-0005.

For orders other than individual consumers, Teri Woods Publishing grants a discount on the purchase of twenty or more copies of a single title order for special markets or premium use.

For orders purchased through the P.O. Box, Teri Woods Publishing offers a 25% discount off the sale price for orders being shipped to prisons, including, but not limited to, federal, state, and county.

Published by Teri Woods Publishing

DEADLY REIGNS

III

THE THIRD OF A TRILOGY

Published by Teri Woods Publishing

Deadly Reigns III, Teri Woods Publishing

Published by:
TERI WOODS PUBLISHING
P.O. Box 20069
New York, NY 10001-0005
www.teriwoodspublishing.com

ISBN: 0-9773234-3-9
Copyright: Will Be Supplied
Library of Congress Catalog Card No: 2009905654

DEADLY REIGNS CREDITS
Story by Curtis Smith and Ginger Laine
Written by Ginger Laine
Edited by Teri Woods and Jessica Tyler
Text formation by Teri Woods

Printed in the USA.

Deadly Reigns III, Teri Woods Publishing

Acknowledgements: My Family always, my moms, Carol, Jess Money, my two sons 'can't sit down' and 'can't listen', my brothers, my secretary Tracey, Lance, and all my great family and great friends in the world who are there for me as much as anyone could ever be, you make my life great!

To everyone that supports my work, I feel connected knowing that we're on the same page. And that connection with you and me is really priceless, ride with that. Thanks for the support, my love always.

Chapter One

"They're all niggers, they are all in it together, every single last one of them," Don Vincente Pancrazio declared. "After what they did to my brothers, I say that we should kill them all like giant cockroaches."

Don Tito Bonafacio leaned forward in his seat and nodded. "I agree, with Don Pancrazio. Damian's father-in-law should be made to suffer. This monkey thinks that he is immune to punishment, just because he is a big fish in some third world shithole. Well, we're gonna prove to him that he's wrong."

The Old Ones gathered around the conference table all nodded in agreement. Today, Don Vincente Pancrazio, Don Tito Bonafacio, Don Salvatore Tiziano, Don Anastasio Crencenzo, Don Luigi Gianchetta and Don Carlo Cinzia were all present. The only New York don not in attendance was Don Graziella Biaggio, who was home nursing a bad cold. The dons had come together for one reason. There would be punishment for Damian's father-in-law, Minister Malaika. The worst mistake that man could have ever made was to send his assassins after them and to murder in cold blood their own family members and loved ones, Don Marcellino Pancrazio, Don Teodosio Pancrazio, Don Gianpaulo Cipriano, and Don Nicostrato Cinzia. Minister Malaika entered into a conflict which he knew little about. Now, the Old Ones were determined to make him pay for his mistake.

Today's meeting was being held in Atlantic City. The New York Old Ones controlled the hotels and casinos there, despite the fact that they were physically located in New Jersey. It had been a source of tension since the first casino had opened its doors, but today, they were all unified.

"And what about Damian and Dante, do you think they will just sit by after we whack the father-in-law?" Don Tiziano asked, blowing rings of cigar smoke into the air.

"Who gives a shit about what they think? Those niggers think they can do anything they want," Don Pancrazio shouted. "Fuck them, fuck their little Commission! I say we hit them first, and hit them hard enough for them to get the message!"

Don Anastasio Crencenzo thumped the ashes from his cigar into his astray. "Vincente's right. No more pussy footing around with these fucking moulees. It's time to put them back in the zoo."

"Let's all be clear about this my friends," Bonafacio told them. "They will come after us, if we hit the father-in-law," said Bonafacio trying to stay on track. Their beef was with Minister Malaika, hitting the Reigns family wasn't in the best interest in his opinion.

"I don't think so," Don Tiziano interjected. "Damian doesn't give a fuck about his father-in-law. And he knows that the old man started this shit, and he knows that he was in the wrong. We all know that Damian's one smart moulee. He's about business, if nothing else."

"Are you saying that we don't hit Damian?" Pancrazio asked, lifting any eyebrow, as he looked over at Tito.

"I'm saying that we could whack the father-in-law, and see what moves the Reigns family makes," Don Bonafacio explained. "That would keep an unnecessary war from jumping off."

Tiziano shook his head. "No, we need to hit them. No

more rationalizing, no more walking on eggs. We hit them, and we hit them hard! That's the only way these monkeys will finally get the message!"

Don Luigi Gianchetta nodded. "I agree, it should be done. The question is, how? What are you proposing, Vincente?"

"I have contacted our cousins in Sicily, and made them aware of the situation," Pancrazio told them. "They are in full agreement with us, that something must be done. They are willing to send us soldiers, money, political help, whatever we need to get our message across."

The dons around the table nodded their approval.

"And how do you intend to catch this father-in-law of theirs?" Bonafacio asked. "He's better protected than the president."

"We have good news my friends. It seems that my loyal and trusting confidants have supplied me with Minister Malaika's itinerary. We now know all his speaking engagements, even his schedule for travel. We know every where he will be for the next six months. We can get him any time we want," smiled Pancrazio. "But first, we need to take out the Reigns family's muscle," Pancrazio added.

"And how are you going to kill off that many soldiers?" Bonafacio asked. "They have thousands of men working for them."

"We don't need to kill off their soldiers, we just need to kill off their top general," Pancrazio explained. "We kill that nuisance of them all, Dante, and the rest of the family is nothing."

"And the sister?" Tiziano asked.

"No, we just need to kill Dante," Pancrazio told them. "We kill him, the others will make peace. He's the muscle of that family. The others are weak."

"I believe you are underestimating the sister," Bonafacio told them, playing devil's advocate.

"No, we get rid of Dante, they are weak," Pancrazio chimed in already having other plans for Princess.

"My dead brother, Nicostrato, God rest his soul, told me that we should have hit those niggers a long time ago," Don Carlo Cinzia told the others. "We should have never let them get so strong! And this Commission too!"

"We are going to take care of that as well," Pancrazio reassured him. "We are going to hit those niggers on all fronts, politically, and economically. As we speak, my people are developing a new contact at the FDA."

"The FDA?" Don Luigi Gianchetta snickered. "What are you going to do, poison all of the chicken and watermelon?"

The dons around the table laughed.

"Although that might just be the best idea I've heard thus far, my friend, I had something else in mind."

"And what is that?" Gianchetta asked.

"Remember, it is the FDA that gives drug approvals," Pancrazio explained. "No more drug approvals, and Bio One is just a bunch of fucking buildings, draining money. Gentlemen, we are going to go after Bio One, and we are going to bankrupt the Reigns family. I want to send their asses right back to the ghetto."

Don Gianchetta leaned forward. "When are the cousins coming in from Sicily?"

"I will make the call," Pancrazio smiled.

"Here?" Tiziano lifted an eyebrow passing him the phone.

The dons sat silently as they watched the call be placed.

"Hello, Fabrizio, this is Vincente. Yes, yes, everything is fine. No, but we are ready. We are ready for you. It is time for you to do what you do best. In 10 hours, I will have a private plane waiting for you at the airport." The others watched as he finished the call and hung up the phone.

Pancrazio turned to his colleagues sitting before him.

"It is done my friends. The wheels are already set in motion." He raised his glass as the others around the table raised theirs.

"To new beginnings," said Vincente Pancrazio.

"To the destruction of the Reigns family, and that bastard father-in-law of theirs," Don Luigi Gianchetta added.

"To the power of the families," Don Tiziano told them.

"To the families!" the dons cheered. "And to Sicily!"

"Sicily!"

Chapter Two

Dante and Angela bumped into one another as he was rushing into the bathroom and she was rushing out of it.

"Dante, ouch, my foot."

Dante stopped for a quick second, looked at his wife with all seriousness and said, "Angela, please we're running late, you must move your big feet out of the way."

"My big feet, my feet are a perfect size seven. Maybe you should move your feet out the way," she said smiling back at her husband as he kissed the tip of her nose. "Mmm hmm, don't start nothing."

"I kissed your nose, Angie."

"That's all it takes, she said slipping on a red Valentino and jiggling her boobies as she maneuvered her breasts perfectly inside the dress.

"Dante, can you please..."

He turned around as Angela flung her hair across her shoulders and out of her face.

"What, do I look okay?" she asked.

Dante silently stared at his wife. She was the most beautiful woman he had ever met in his life. So beautiful that it was moments like these her beauty would sweep him right off his feet.

"Angela, we are running late. Why don't you get one of the maids to help you dress? Don't you see me trying to shave," he deliberately asked wanting desperately to rip her dress off and take her right there on the bathroom counter.

"Oh, Dante, you are such a prune," she uttered before fluttering down the hall. He could hear her calling out for Niurka, a young Spanish girl who had been hired to be Angela's companion or what some would call a home assistant.

By the time he was ready, Angela had been touched over with a fine tooth comb. From the top of her head to the tips of her feet, everything was perfect. Her makeup, stunning to say the least, her dress, absolutely the most beautiful gown that would be worn in the building, and her skin, glowing as if somewhere inside her burned a fire. She was picture-perfect, flawless in every sense of the word wearing over three million dollars of her own personal jewelry.

"Dante, do I loo..."

She couldn't get out the sentence because standing before her, Dante opened a small carrying case containing a diamond necklace with a large ruby heart surrounded by diamonds. It looked just like the heart of the ocean, only red.

"Oh Dante," she gasped reaching for the precious stone as Dante slammed the carrying case closed, the sound startling her a bit.

"Dante, stop, this isn't something to play here, not

with me," she said her eyes piercing his.

Dante opened the case, gently placed the necklace in his hand, walked behind Angela and fastened the clasp around her neck.

"Perfect, the necklace is absolutely perfect on you. Come, let's go, we are running late and my brother is going to kill me if I'm not there for him."

The gala was being held on the Bio One campus, inside of their grand ball room. The ballroom was a two thousand diameter glass dome that had been constructed to host the companies numerous charity events, media gatherings, and company balls. Tonight, all of Texas's most powerful and prominent were in attendance.

Cherin King shifted the wireless microphone into her right hand and lifted it to her lips.

"Tonight, it is my distinct pleasure, to introduce you to our host, Bio One's chairman and founder, Mr. Damian Reigns!"

The crowd broke into a steady thunderous applause, as Damian made his way across the stage, and accepted the microphone. He waved his hand, "Thank you, thank you, thank you," he said trying to calm the crowd to a hush.

"Tonight, you are about to witness history," Damian Reigns announced. "You can all say that you were present, this evening for one of the most important announcements in the history of biotechnology."

The ballroom had grown eerily silent.

"Tonight, it is with great pleasure that I announce to you, the formal alliance between The University of Texas Health Science Center, Sea World Center, and Bio One!"

The crowd broke into rapturous applause. Damian allowed them to applaud for several minutes, before calming them once again.

"Imagine if you will the genetic mapping of every

known species in the ocean and learning the secrets of the deep and applying a wide range of biologics that will lead to a host of cures from cancer, diabetes, heart disease, to even Alzheimer's. The possibilities are now endless. Charting the human genome was just the beginning, now we are truly embarking on a new frontier and Bio One will charter the genome of every creature in the sea, which will launch us on a voyage of medical progress unheard of in human history. We are about to begin, a new age of discovery. And our new alliances will create powerful synergies, coordinate research and resources, streamline paperwork, foster technology sharing, and lead to a hosts of new discoveries. Ladies and Gentlemen, welcome to a new age of discovery!"

The crowd erupted into a non-stop thunderous applause even more rapturous than the preceding one.

"The reason you are all gathered here tonight, is to witness the final application process in which we will request the release of RD-221, and RDX-214. We have developed a gene based cure for cancerous cells in the human body. Ladies and gentlemen, welcome RD-221 and RDX-214, ladies and gentlemen, welcome to the cure for cancer."

Again, the crowd broke into a rapturous applause.

"Previously, all of our research was focused on the cartilage of sea life mammals as being an angiogenesis inhibitor. However, once we changed our focus to the epigonal organ in sharks, and its hem poetic functions, we were able to map out its T-Cell differentiation processes, and identify the specific hemocells that act as pathogen detoxifiers. What we also found, were cells that not only acted as angiogenin inhibitors, retarding the growth of new blood vessels to feed to tumors, but cells that act as broad spectrum serum antibodies that actively attack any cellular corruption of all organs and tissues. We have traced these serum antibodies' anti-corruption functions, as far back as the gastrulation stage. Ladies and gentlemen, what we have

9

achieved here, through bio genetic research, is a process that leaps past stem cell manipulation, and all of its political, ethical, and moral quandaries, and allows for immediate, safe, and affordable treatment, of not only cancerous cells, but a variety of cellular ailments. Ladies and gentlemen, we have conducted testing, using RDX-214 that took a person with a human immune-deficiency virus or HIV, and restored their resistance, using broad spectrum serum antibodies. Yes, we are on the cusp, of a cure for AIDS just as well."

The audience gasped, and then broke into wild applause.

"Ladies and gentlemen, we have moved beyond the level of molecular biology, past nano technology, to levels of nano molecular structures. We are on the cusp of a new era of learning and exploration. Once again, I welcome you to project Nemisis, welcome to the foundation of The Bio One Nemisis Project Group, welcome, to a new beginning!"

Damian handed the microphone back to Cherin King one of his attorneys, and walked off the stage to handshakes, cheers, pats-on-the-back, hugs, congratulations, and well-wishes. He spied his brother on the far side of the room, and quickly made his way through the crowd to join him.

"You are the biggest fucking nerd I've ever met," Dante told him, shaking his hand. "I didn't understand a word you were saying."

Damian laughed and hugged his brother.

"That's it," Dante continued. "If you're not going to be speaking English, this is the last one of these things I'm attending."

"I was speaking English," Damian smiled.

"No, you were speaking nerd," Dante told him.

"Oh my, is that Angela?"

Dante and Damian both looked across the floor as they couldn't help but to see Angela shaking hands and greeting some of Texas most elite socialites.

"Yes, that is Angela."

"Stunning, simply stunning is all I have to say."

"Brother, are you eyeing your sister-in-law. Wouldn't that be like some distant relative act of incest?" He looked at Damian and realized he was really checking Angela out. "I'm supposed to be able to trust you, brother. My God stop drooling at her, stop staring at my wife and go give another one of your boring speeches to a bunch of boring people that understand you." Dante and Damian both watched as Angela glided across the floor and approached them.

"Damian, my dear sweet brother-in-law, how are you?" Angela asked as Damian grabbed her waist, embraced her closely, spun her around as if a dancing doll, kissing her cheek ever so lightly as he smoothly glided her back to where she started.

"I saw that," murmured Dante.

"Saw what?" Damian asked as he winked at Angela.

"Yes, Dante, what did you see?" Angela replied as she winked back at Damian.

"I see every unseen line and I hear every unspoken word, never forget that," he said deeply believing that they both secretly admired one another.

"May I have this dance?" Damian asked graciously extending his hand.

"How could I say no to the founding father of the cure for cancer?" Angela laughed as she placed her hand ever so gently into Damian's.

"Do you mind, brother, may I have this dance with your wife?"

"No, she's my wife and you certainly may not."

"Oh, Dante, stop being a prune."

"Yes, Dante, stop being a prune," smiled Damian.

"Of course we must, come Damian, let's dance," said Angela as she patted her husband's heavy chest and lead Damian to the dance floor. *You Look Wonderful Tonight* was being sung by Michael Buble as Stevie J played piano, with a full orchestra conducted by Dexter Wansel. Damian had spared no expense in planning tonight's event. He made it perfectly clear that he wanted nothing but the best.

"Excuse me, may I cut in?" asked Dante in less than five mintues, standing behind his brother.

"And to say no would be rude," he said frowning his face at his brother's timing. Then he added, "Angela, such a vision of loveliness, thank you for this dance," said Damian as he slightly bent his head and kissed Angela's hand before letting his brother take over.

"You are such a wus, you do know that Dante. You married a wus, Angela."

"Of course I know, but I do love him so," she smiled at her husband as Dante suddenly spun her around and forcefully pulled her back into his arms.

"I got a wus for you," he whispered dancing her away.

"Really, and I have a pus for you," she teased.

"Now you're talking."

"No, darling, seriously, I feel like I've taken suddenly ill. Not quite myself, but yet all here, nauseous but starving. I can't explain it. Will you take me home?"

"Damian will kill us."

"I know, but really, I don't feel myself. I want to lie down."

"With me?"

"Of course, darling Dante, with only you," she smiled and Dante knew it was time to go.

Dante spoke with his brother as Angela sat waiting for him patiently sipping a ginger ale. Her stomach felt queasy and she suddenly felt exhausted. She watched her husband as he made his way over to her and helped her put on her fur coat.

"You're so good to me, Dante."

"How can I not be, Ange? How could any man not be?"

Dante clasped his wife's arm, and led her out of the ballroom to their brand new Bentley Continental Flying Spur.

For the trip home, Dante decided to take the highway. Normally, for security purposes, he wouldn't take the same way home that he took to his destination. But tonight, his wife was sick, and he wanted to get her home as soon as possible. Besides, he was in Texas, in his own hometown and he had a car full of bodyguards following behind him. What could happen?

The Hydra 70 rocket from the light anti-tank weapon that took out his bodyguards quickly made him regret his decision and now, his car full of bodyguards following behind him to protect him and his wife were gone.

Dante mashed his accelerator, propelling the Bentley and picking up speed giving distance to them and the assassins. The light from the second rocket flying just in front of his vehicle was blinding. It came from the side, passed right by them less than a yard from the car. He swerved losing control of the car and crashed into an eighteen wheeler that was traveling in the next lane. The eighteen wheeler's tires sent the Bentley bouncing back into the concrete divider, which caused the car to bounce back into the Mack truck. Dante hit his brakes, before the deadly ping pong effect sent his vehicle beneath the tires of the massive tractor trailer truck. He skidded in the middle of the highway for quite some distance, before bringing his vehicle to a complete stop.

The Bentley stopped in the middle of the highway and that stop allowed the assassins to catch up to it. They skidded to a halt just a short distance from the badly banged up Bentley, and poured from their black Hummer H2 with fully automatic weapons to finish what they had started.

Inside of the Bentley, Angela pulled out her pistol, while Dante tried to get the car's damaged gears to lock into place.   She rolled down the cracked, but not broken, armored passenger window, and fired her weapon at the hit team.   She dropped two of them within three seconds, causing the other's to take cover and fire.

Angela quickly rolled her window back up, allowing the armored glass to shield them from the onslaught of automatic fire. The bullets from the hit teams AR-15 assault rifles raked across the window and body of the cars, sending sparks flying everywhere.

"Will you get us the hell outta here?!" Angela shouted.

"What do you think I'm trying to do?!" Dante shouted back.

He leaned his seat back, and scooted back, so that he could get his leg into position.

"Dante, they're readying another rocket!" Angela shouted putting in another clip to ready her Walther.

Dante kicked as hard as he could, sending the gear shifter into reverse. He then hopped back into the driver's position and hit the gas, sending the car speeding into reverse. Dante turned the steering wheel, whipping the car around, and began flying down the highway driving backwards.

They could see the flash and bright exhaust from the rocket as it flew past them.

"They're hopping back into their truck!" Angela shouted.

"Let's see if this thing works now," Dante told her. He spun the Bentley around, and pulled down on the gear shifter, sending the car into drive. "Yes!" He hit the gas, and quickly accelerated to nearly two hundred miles per hour.

Dante never saw the forth rocket that the assassins fired at him. It struck just below the armored Bentley, sending it flipping forward through the air, and then off of a nearby embankment where it flipped over three times before landing upside down.

"Angela," Dante called out as he looked over at his wife, blinked one time and lost consciousness.

Chapter Three

Dante rolled over in his hospital bed to find his sister reading *Chances* a Jackie Collins novel stationed next to him.

"Princess," he whispered.

"I'm here, Dante, I'm here brother and I won't leave you. Don't say anything, everything is fine, you are going to be okay, you're in the hospital, just close your eyes and rest. I won't let anything happen to you."

For some strange reason his sister's words gave him comfort. Any other time, he'd be calling for security, but not today. Today, he knew his sister was there to protect and nurture him, not harm him and she was actually just as good at being nice as she was being her normal, nasty, evil self. And for the strangest moment hearing the sound of his sister's voice eased him like rocking a baby back to sleep and he closed his eyes and he was safe. Dante did not wake, fully that is for another 72 hours. He suffered minor injuries, however, he had a real bad concussion and for many days he was unconscious. But, when he did wake, the first person he asked for was Angela. Princess looked at her brother and then looked away.

"Princess, where is Angela?" he demanded from her once again, this time in his fashionable Reigns tone and demeanor setting the stage for an immediate response.

"Dante," she said as she turned to face him, her face telling a horrid truth.

"What, Princess, is she dead?" he asked already knowing the answer from the look on his sister's face.

"Dante, please, you should rest."

"Answer me, Princess God damn you, answer me, now," he demanded reaching for his nurse button.

"Dante, Angela, was hurt, really really bad. She's in a coma, a vegetative state and she's paralyzed Dante from the neck down. The doctor's feel she'll never walk again, and they say that the chances of her coming out of the coma are around 2 maybe 3%. I'm so sorry, brother. I'm so sorry," Princess couldn't help but to wipe tears off her face. She quickly turned away from her brother and picked up a tissue and wiped her eyes not wanting her mascara to run. "She's on life support, and everyone has been waiting for you to decide what to do with her."

Dante sat back in his hospital bed. He was speechless and his body went numb. His heart was sinking fast, *not Angela, please not Angela.* His mind searched her every smile, her every kiss, her every touch. *Not my soul mate.*

He immediately wanted to see her.

"Dante, I don't think that would be good. I think you need your rest."

"I said, I want to see her god dammit, Princess, I need you, can't you see that!" he screamed at her demanding she do as he said. "Please, just take me to her, please."

"Of course, Dante, of course," she walked out the room and quickly returned with a wheelchair.

"Let me help you."

Princess treated her brother as if he was the most precious thing on earth. She touched him with her gentle hands and helped him get into the wheelchair. She gently placed both his feet in the holders and began to wheel him down the hall to the elevators. They took the elevator to the third floor as Princess wheeled her brother to the ICU where Angela was being monitored.

"Um, I'm sorry visiting hours are over," said an unknowing nurse.

Princess could see the look of unrest in her brother's face and she quickly placed her hand on her brother's shoulder. "I will take care of this."

Princess moved the nurse away from her brother, returned seconds later and began to stroll Dante down the rows of beds to where Angela was laying.

Angela had tubes sticking out of what seemed to be every part of her body. Her mouth was plugged up with a tube stretching into her esophagus, her neck had a thick, large brace that seemed to hold her entire body together and even though her eyes were open, they seemed to flicker in and out of some far away place, never once responding to anything or anyone since the accident.

"Oh god," was all Dante could muster. He covered his mouth in awe as he looked at his lifeless wife.

"Has anyone called her parents?"

"I've already contacted them. I sent Air Reigns One to pick them up. They should be here in the morning.

"Can I have a moment, Princess...alone with my wife, please?"

"Dante, of course, I'll be right over there." Princess pointed to a waiting area near the nurse's station and walked over and took a seat as she watched her brother from across the floor.

She couldn't hear her brother, but then again, she didn't need to. She already knew that Dante was pleading for her life, for a miraculous miracle to bring her back. And it was his pleas that brought tears to her eyes. She never thought she'd see her brother broken, that more than anything was heartbreaking enough. But to have to witness what Dante was going through, was pure hell. And to know that he'd break bread with Satan himself if it would bring Angela back was an even more dreaded thought. Deep down inside, she knew that there was no way humanly possible that Angela would come back. She was a shell holding her spirit hostage. To give her peace, was what her brother would have to do. The question is would he be able to pull the cord. *Of course he will, after all he is a Reigns,* Princess couldn't help but to think that if she were in her brother's shoes, what she would do. *Of course, pull the plug.*

It was at that moment, Angela's mother and father walked into the ICU room. Princess knew exactly who they were. A nurse walked over to them and Princess listened to the father as he spoke with the nurse.

"We're here to see our daughter, Angela Paxton Reigns," Angela's father requested, looking tired and worn. Both he and his wife had not slept, since receiving the news of Angela and Dante's accident. Mr. and Mrs. Paxton only had Angela, their one child. She was her father's pride and her mother's joy. Every waking moment of her childhood had been spent doting on her and making sure she had everything she needed. Angela had attended St. Mary's Catholic School for Girls, the best private Catholic school her father's money could afford. Everyday, Angela would come home from school, do her homework, and then help her mother set the table for dinner. She'd even do the dishes, help with laundry and make her own bed before leaving for school each day. Angela was always a wonderful daughter. She excelled in high school, joining the ROTC program, and graduating with honors, then on to Fisk University where she graduated Summa Cum Laude and made the

President's List all four years in a row, then onto Princeton. After college, she joined the military and finally ended her career with the Secret Service after marrying Dante. Her father looked across the floor and saw Dante sitting next to her bed.

"Excuse me, sir," said Princess extending her hand. "My name is Princess, Princess Reigns. My brother is with her. Come, have a seat for just a few moments," she said as she smiled and led the family to sit down with her in the waiting area.

"So, how was the flight in?" asked Princess making small talk.

"It was amazing. I've never seen an aircraft like that in my life," responded Angela's mother making small talk with Angela's sister-in-law.

"I'm sorry," said Mr. Paxton as he rose to his feet. "I need to see my little girl," he said wanting to see his baby. He began walking over to where Dante sat beside her bed as Mrs. Paxton, jumped up and followed her husband.

It seemed as though a police whistle blew and froze them dead in their tracks.

"Mrs. Paxton," said Princess and she placed her hand on the older woman's shoulder. "Are you alright?"

"Oh, my god, no, no, not Angela," her mother cried out as she fell into the arms of her husband.

"Mr. Paxton, I'm so sorry," said Princess as she patted him on the back and then turned Dante's wheelchair to face them.

"Howard, Mary, I'm so glad you're here," said Dante.

"What happened to her?" asked Mr. Paxton.

"We had a car accident." Dante looked off into space not saying another word. Angela's parents looked at him, then at each other.

"You will have to forgive my brother," said Princess. "He still isn't himself."

Angela's mother sat on the other side of the bed,

holding Angela's hand, rubbing the hair from her face and kissing her forehead.

"The doctor's are asking that the family make a unison decision as to what needs to be done from here," said Princess. "I know this is hard for you all, however, we should let them know something this evening."

"What kind of decision?" asked Mary.

"Umm...the life support, the doctor wants to know the family's decision, whether to leave her connected to the life support system or not."

"I have already spoken to the doctor. We will unplug the cord tomorrow," said Dante not one crack in his voice or look of emotion in his eyes.

"Howard, please, no, don't let him, Howard," pleaded Angela's mother.

"Wait a minute, tomorrow."

"Yes, sir, first thing in the morning," answered Dante. "I will pull the cord at day break, when the tip of the sun begins to rise over the earth."

"Would that be after your morning cup of coffee or before?" asked Angela's father weary and irate.

"Come again?"

"You're talking about pulling the plug on Angela, our daughter. Why? Where's your faith. How do you know she won't come back?"

"The doctors, Howard, they are how I know. And even if she did come back, don't you think life in this bed would be a bit cruel, just a bit unfair for her. Angela had zest, Angela loved life, she loved living her life. This isn't living, it could never be," said Dante as he looked down at her shaking his head, "This isn't living."

"That's murder, Howard, we can't let him pull the plug on our baby. Please, Dante, please just have a little faith, don't end her life. Don't do that," pleaded Mrs. Paxton as she begged him for her daughter's life.

Faith, geez, are they serious? Dante knew they would never understand, never. And how could they? It was their daughter, their precious baby girl. He understood. However, it didn't change anything. And now that they were here to say goodbye, he would pull the plug in the morning.

"Princess, can you take me back to my room please. I'd like to get my rest. We have a busy day tomorrow." He then turned to the Paxtons, "Goodnight."

"Goodnight," added Princess as she pushed her brother's wheelchair out the ICU.

Chapter Four

The Paxtons had wasted so much energy and so much breath that by the time the sun was fixin' to rise, they were too tired and too cried out to fight with Dante or his methodic sister.

"No, you can't, you just can't, Dante! She's my baby," screamed Mary Paxton as she charged towards Dante, pouncing on him, as she slapped his face and chest. It took all of everyone, but Howard most of all to contain her.

"I'm so sorry, Dante," he said hoping his wife hadn't offended him.

He sat calmly in his wheelchair brushing off his shoulders. "It's fine, Howard, I understand. I do." *Mother-in-law or not, if she jumps me again, I'm having her dealt with.* He couldn't help but thinking to himself how Howard would have no wife and no child, if Mary kept attacking him and of course she did. All night long, she even came into his room after Princess had gone home and tried to talk reason to him, but it didn't work. There was just no way, Dante would allow his wife to be an invalid, unable to walk, stand, eat or go to the bathroom. No, that would never be. Angela was too strong to be weak, a fighter, not handicapped and in his heart, he knew it was what Angela would want.

Dante had made up his mind and there was nothing they could do about it, even though they were Angela's parents. He was her husband and whether they liked it or not, he had the final say over what would be done.

With everyone gathered around the bed, Mary Paxton reached for her daughter's hand and began to pray. Her father stood at the foot of her bed as tears streamed down his face. Dante was ready to pull the electrical cord from its outlet and bring Angela the closure she much deserved.

"Mr. Reigns, wait! May I speak with you?"

Dante looked up and followed the voice of interruption, "Yes, doctor, everything okay?" he said dropping the plug as if on cue.

"Yes, Mr. Reigns, just one minute."

Princess looked at the doctor as he spoke to Dante. *What now?* She wondered to herself, knowing that by the look on her brother's face, something was up.

Dante walked back over to Angela's bed where the family was gathered.

"The doctor just informed me that Angela is with child. An examination and blood work confirmed that she is pregnant. The doctor is going to schedule an ultrasound to confirm how far along she is."

"Dante, what does this mean?" asked Princess, concerned for the baby's well being.

"The doctor said she can incubate the child while in a vegetative state. Her body will do all the work, even if she's not conscious, we can still have a healthy, normal baby," he said all the while hoping and praying the child would be healthy, but more importantly, hoping and praying the child would be a boy.

"Thank you Jesus, I knew it, I knew it. I just knew it. See, I told you Dante, I told you. You don't know faith, but I do. Thank, you Jesus, thank you. My baby will be back. I know she will, she's coming back and you won't pull no cord on her, you just won't. See, see how he works, see how glorious God is?" said Mary Paxton as she cried tears of joy as her and Howard hugged one another.

Chapter Five

Dante calmly walked into the living room of Princess's mansion. "I'm killing them all, just so you know!"

Princess smiled. "I already imagined that. How's Angela, any change?"

"No, she's still the same. She's scheduled for an ultrasound to make sure the baby is okay and see how far pregnant she is."

"It's wonderful, another Reigns, right Damian," said Princess trying to sound optimistic.

"Really, Dante, I'm so happy for you," Damian said, trying to calm his brother.

"No!" Dante shouted.

"No, what?" Damian asked.

"No! Patronizing me isn't going to work, just know that," Dante snapped at them.

"Know what?" Damian asked.

"You are not going to be reasonable and logical, in an attempt to stop me!" Dante barked. "They are dead! And there's nothing you can say or do to stop me! They tried to kill me, with my wife in the car! My pregnant wife! What if I had pulled that plug, Damian."

"But you didn't, you didn't pull the plug, and the baby will be fine."

"Besides Dante, think clearly, you and I know that

Angela's not a civilian, and they know it too," Princess said calmly. "She's a legitimate target, Dante, a very legitimate target, be she your wife or pregnant."

"Well, they're all legitimate targets too. Aren't they?" he asked making sure that Princess and Damian were standing on the right side of the fence.

"Dante, I'm not going to stop you from doing what you feel you have to do," Damian told him. "But still, we have to think things through."

"What is there to think about?" Dante asked.

"We have to plan," Damian told him. "You can't be reckless not with the Old Ones. You know this already."

"Damian's right, big brother," Princess told him. "They hit you for a reason. That reason being they see you as the head, the strength and they fear you, they fear you the most."

"And what's that got to do with Angela?"

"Everything!" Princess shouted at him as she slammed down a Faberge 24k gold trimmed egg she used as a pill holder. "It has everything to do with Angela." She said inspecting her egg, making sure she hadn't broken it. That hit against the two of you is only the beginning. The Old Ones are planning something much bigger, much bigger than we probably would give them the credit for. Pay attention, Dante. Don't let what has happened to Angela deter you from the art of war, which you are absolutely a genius at."

"She's right, Dante. The Old Ones are up to something. Hitting you was just the beginning. And to hit you means that all of the Old Ones had to give their consent. And they crept into our backyard, like snakes, now that takes a lot of balls. It's the Old Ones. They want a war."

"You would think they would have gone after Minister Malaika or Damian and Illyassa for that matter, wouldn't you Dante?" questioned Princess as she decided to stir up the pot.

Damian looked at his brother wishing that it was he and Illyassa that was hit, instead of Dante and Angela. He actually smiled at the thought.

"It doesn't matter. What is done is done. Now, it's time to take action and give them back what they have started," Dante declared.

"We will," Damian nodded.

"You two need to bring Damian's father-in-law up to speed," Princess told them.

"Why?" Damian asked not wanting to deal with the man any more than he wanted to deal with his new bride.

"He started this shit, he has men in-country, and he needs to commit a considerable amount of resources to this war. Why in the world should the Reigns family pay for this war?" Princess explained.

"She's right," Dante declared. "Your father in-law would want to contribute. It's his stupid fault. God damn it Damian, why did you marry her again because I'm ready to kill her too," shouted Dante forgetting his brother's own personal sacrifices. Damian was coaxed by Stacia to marry Illyassa to free Dante. They needed the power of the Minister and now that power had come back to haunt them. But the thought of Dante killing Illyassa again made Damian smile.

"What are you smiling about?" Princess asked confused.

"Yeah, why do you look like that?" asked Dante.

"Nothing, just a thought," he said shaking it off. "Dante, I'm sorry for Angela. It's not my fault, I would never cause you or Angela harm. I love her too Dante."

Of course Damian wouldn't do anything to Angela or to him. He was his brother's keeper. Damian embraced his brother and whispered in his ear. Princess watched as if still five, hating the bond they shared even from so long ago. He let his brother go.

"I will do whatever you want me to do." He pierced

Dante's eyes with his own then lowered his head and nodded.

"This thing is going to turn into one big mess," Princess declared, while shaking her head. "And that wife of yours..."

"What about her?" Damian asked hoping and praying he had an ally in her with Dante throwing accusations his way.

"A problem," Princess told him. "She's in California trying to be an actress, you're in Texas fucking around, she's going to be a problem. And if one of your little love trysts ever become public, and she finds out about it, she's going to be very upset. One little crying spell to daddy, and we're going to have fucking Ethiopian assassins roaming around Texas. I'm telling you, she's going to be a problem."

"I can handle her," Damian told her.

No, you can't but I can and I will, Princess thought to herself.

"In the meantime, I want everyone to stick to the plan."

"Which plan is that?" Dante asked.

"We're pulling out of the Commission, and we're moving away from sales, to distribution," Damian explained. "Are we all clear on this?"

Dante and Princess nodded.

"One more thing," Princess told him.

"What's that?" Damian asked.

"If they are bold enough to start hitting us here and if they're going after family members, then perhaps we should make alternate living arrangements," Princess suggested.

"What type of alternate arrangements would you be suggesting?" Damian asked.

"We should all stick together," Princess told him.

"Like move in together?" Dante frowned wondering what his kid sister had up her sleeve. *Live with Princess, is she crazy? She had me do a free fall from a giant skyscraper. She's a fucking nut case, a higher level of psychotic, dillusioned.*

"It'll free up our men to do other things. Instead of having bodyguards at three separate mansions, plus Mom's place, we can have them at just one. We need to make sure that mom is safe," she said with confidence knowing that no one would disagree to that.

"I agree. We should move everyone into the ranch. We can protect everyone a lot better that way. Plus, we can see someone coming from miles away there. It's all the way up on the hills."

"And mom will love it. She'll have all three of her one and onlies," Princess said smiling.

"I don't know, mom might not go for it," thought Damian out loud.

"Of course she will, we can make it seem like we're all just concerned about her health."

"She's right, mom would love it," chimed in Dante. "On one order, the house is a safe zone for all of us, agreed," he asked specifically looking at his sister, Damian eyeing her as well.

"God, Dante, we are not at war, what is wrong with you?" She looked away from him and focused on Damian. "You too? Oh, please, I'd never," she said smiling seductively.

"What about this birthday party?" asked Damian.

"What birthday party?" questioned Dante.

"Dajon and Anjoinette are throwing a party for Cheyenne at the ranch. No one told you because no one wanted to bother you with it. The guest list has been verified. We have our security detail dressing up like clowns and super heroes, I told Mina and Brandon to tone it down as much as possible."

"We get through this weekend at the ranch, and after that, it's business," Damian said. "Dante, are you with me?"

"After this weekend, the gloves come off," Dante

directly ordered.

"After this weekend, the gloves will come off," Damian reassured him.

Dante nodded. He was ready for war.

Chapter Six

The Reigns Ranch

Emory Reigns walked across the Brazilian Cherry floors of her thirty thousand square foot plantation style mansion, to her stainless steel Sub Zero refrigerator, and pulled out a bottle of Evian water. She unscrewed the cap and gently took a swig.

Her children had summoned her for a meeting.

"Mother, Thursday, precisely at noon, mark it, don't forget," she cradled the thought in her mind, recalling her daughter's orders. *God only knows what they want now,* she thought to herself. It was always something with the three of them, always had been. Ever since they were little it was always something. Dante being the oldest always wanted attention and being the first born got what ever he wanted. Damian being the second child, was stuck in the middle, and over shadowed by Dante. Still, he grew into a great and powerful man. Damian never needed much, was always off to the side, alone in his own world, with his thoughts. *He was always a scientist,* thought Emory at the sight of Damian today in his short, white, over-coat and eye goggles looking like the little boy he once was. And of course, the enchanted Diamora, who hated her name and made everyone call her Princess when she was five years old. "I won't answer you.

My name is Princess, and that's what you better call me or else." She could hear Princess now squealing at her brothers, especially Darius, her youngest. Princess picked on him so bad because he was small, more so than Dante and Damian, because they were bigger than her, even still she gave them a run for their money as well. She had so many wonderful memories and she could see their lives, even her husband's, flash before her eyes. They were the cutest and most innocent bunch when they were small. *But they're not little anymore and they are far from innocent,* Emory couldn't help but to think as she tapped her fingers on her water bottle.

"Ma'am, the pool company is here for service. Should I open the gate for him?"

"Who is it?"

"The pool man, ma'am, he says he's here to clean the pool, but I don't see him on the list."

A long silence filled the air.

"No, the pool company is not on the list for entries today. Maybe there was a mistake. Let me see the camera."

Emory quickly moved into a large foyer and peered at a forty two inch flat screen hanging on the wall and looked at the front gate, four different angles of the front gate, which was a mile from the ranch.

"That's not our pool cleaner. Good Lord, that's not even the company that services the house."

"Yes, ma'am, I'll let Brandon know right away, ma'am," said Selita, a middle aged Spanish woman in her forties. She knew the drill, she had been around the Reigns family for many years and she knew that safety was always a priority for the family.

Emory watched as the guy was escorted away from the cameras, as a security detail hopped into the van and drove it away from the house. *There's no telling what will happen to him,* she thought to herself just as Damian's DB9 pulled up to the gate. And then behind her, a member of

Brandon's security team appeared.

"Madam Reigns, everything is fine, the pool cleaner had the wrong house. We let him go. Everything is fine."

"Oh, that's good news for the day."

"Yes, ma'am for him it certainly is."

Damian walked in the door as he overheard his mother talking to security.

"No need to worry mom, I'm here now and I will save you," he said as he hugged Emory and planted a kiss on her cheek.

"I know, son. I know you will," she smiled back. "How are you?" she asked as they walked back down the hall, hand in hand as if he were five.

"Hi, Selita, you look well," said Princess as she came bursting through the front door. "Where's my mother?" she asked ordering an answer.

"She just went in the sitting room with your brother," answered Selita kindly.

"Here you go," said Princess handing Selita her handbag. "Hold this until I come back."

"Yes ma'am."

And five minutes later, Dante arrived. "Hello, Dante," said Selita as she greeted him coming through the door still holding Princess' bag in her hand.

"Hello Selita, how are you," said Dante welcoming her friendly smile.

"I am fine, and how is your beautiful wife," she asked.

"There's not any change, Selita. Thank you for asking."

"Of course, no need to thank me. Just let me know if you need anything okay, Dante."

"Okay, I'm fine."

He walked down the hall and entered his mother's sitting room. His brother, Damian was sitting next to their mother while Princess sat in the far corner, but somehow was in the middle of it all.

Dante walked over to his mother, kissed her cheek and then sat down in a chair to her right.

"How's Angela, Dante?" his mother asked full of concern.

"She's pregnant, mom. She's still in a coma, and they say her odds aren't good, but she's pregnant and the doctor says the pregnancy is in tact."

"I know about the pregnancy, Princess told me, I think it is wonderful news and with God's grace, she'll come back Dante. We just have to keep Angela in our prayers," she said rubbing Damian's leg. "So, what do you guys have up your sleeves? I'm getting old, but I'm not there, yet. I can tell when you guys are up to something."

"Oh mother, we are up to nothing. We've just made a decision. We want to move back home!"

"You want to move back home?" Emory looked around the room at each of her children, not saying a word, simply looking in their faces. "Is there reason that I should be concerned or are you guys unable to pay your rent?"

"We can pay our rent, mom, you know that," said Damian. We have reason to be concerned for you, for all of us."

"Especially after what has happened to Angela, we don't want to take any chances. Just for a few months. I think we should all be together, especially to all be here for Dante, mother. We just have to make this sacrifice," said Princess, not wanting to expose the threat of war to her mother.

Emory hadn't lived with her children in years. Darius, the youngest had fled the chicken coupe over ten years ago. "Ya'll gonna drive me crazy. Where you think your staying, I know not in the main house. I can't take all that bickering back and forth."

"Mother, there's plenty of space here. I'm taking the West Wing."

"I'll take the East Wing," signed Damian.

"Why don't you stay with mother, Dante. Stay here in the main house. You'd like that wouldn't you mother?" asked Princess.

Is she crazy, I can't live with her, thought Emory.

Princess moved behind the sofa where Emory and Damian were seated and she began to stroke her mother's shoulders as if petting a wounded animal.

"Right mother, you'd like that wouldn't you. You're precious first born penis right here by your side," joked Princess.

"Get off me, Diamora, that's what's wrong with you now," she said slapping Princess' hand away and calling her by her real name, a name Princess detested.

"Eeeww, where'd you get that horrid name from? Don't call me that mother, you know I don't like that name."

"Well, stop messing with me. Dante can go where he wants to. See, this is what I'm talking about. I don't know how you think I'm going to be able to handle all three of you under the same roof. You guys must be kidding."

"No, mommy, I don't want to take any chances," said Dante, his mother's attention now dead set on him.

"Then I guess our business is done here. I can get on with my day," said Emory looking at her Presidential Rolex she was wearing on her left wrist. "It's time for lunch, care to join me, anyone?"

"No, mother I have business to attend," said Princess ready to get on with her day as well.

"I have to do a little toy shopping this afternoon, sorry," said Damian as he kissed his mother's cheek.

"I'll have lunch, mommy," said Dante.

"Of course he will, he's the little mommy's dearest isn't he, Dame?" joked Princess.

"Always has been," said Damian as they made their way down the hall.

"You made her stand there like that," asked Damian as he watched Princess snatch her pocketbook away from Selita without so much as a thank you.

"It's her job," said Princess throwing her pocket book onto the passenger seat of her Continental.

"You've made her do more than hold a pocketbook, not just her, all of these poor Spanish girls around the house. Geez, don't you got nerve," joked Princess as she zoomed away in her Bentley.

Chapter Seven

Damian stood in front of the toy aisle, staring blankly at a couple of dolls. Usually he paid someone to do this sort of thing for him.

"For you?" a soft voice asked.

Damian broke from his trance and turned in the direction from which the voice came. She was the most beautiful woman he had ever seen. At first glance he couldn't tell her nationality. She wore her hair long and flowing down her back, and she had high, very well-pronounced cheekbones, and deep, rich brown eyes. Her beauty cast a spell on him.

"So, which doll interests you the most?" she asked with a smile.

He couldn't even answer the question. That's how beautiful she was. *Look at her body.* Damian shook his head. "None, I mean... I don't know."

She smiled and extended her hand. "Daniella, Daniella Worthington."

"Has anyone ever told you how beautiful you are?"

"Every day, including holidays, weekends and Sunday."

"Unbelievably beautiful," Damian said looking her up

and down. "Have I seen you somewhere before, on the cover of a magazine or something? Is that you in the Victoria Secrets catalog."

"Very funny, no it's not. You never did say your name, though."

Damian clasped her soft, well-manicured hand and shook it. "Dame."

"A pleasure to meet you, Dame," she smiled. "Not often do you normally find grown men in this section."

"My niece, it's her birthday," Damian told her.

"Ahhh, that explains it," Daniella smiled. "And how old is she turning?"

"She turned six today, but we're having a party for her on Saturday," Damian told her. "You're accent..."

"I was born in Jamaica to a Belizean father, and an English mother," Daniella explained. "I was raised in England, university studies at Oxford, Ph.D in New England. My accent is all over the place."

"No, it's actually very beautiful."

"Wow, well thank you."

"So, what brings you in here?" Damian asked.

"I'm sending a present to my niece back in London."

"Birthday?"

Daniella shook her head, "No, just a gift to let her know that I love her and miss her."

"That's very kind."

"I'm a kind and giving person."

"Are you?" Damian smiled. "Kind enough to help a desperate man figure out what a six year old girl would like?"

"I think I could be of some service in that department."

"Thank you!" Damian laughed. "I was totally lost."

"Well, maybe I've found you."

"I hope so," said Damian smiling trying not stare.

"Here, try this one," Daniella told him. She pulled a

doll from the shelf, and handed it to Damian.

"We have a winner!" Damian declared.

Daniella laughed.

"How can I thank you?" Damian asked. "You saved me from an hour of prolonged standing and debating which one to pick."

"You're welcome."

"No, seriously," Damian said. "May I take you to dinner."

"Dinner? Just for picking out a doll? It's not that serious."

"No, I'd love to take you to lunch or dinner."

"Why?"

"Because, when I turned around and saw you, you took my breath away."

"Wow. And I get dinner just for that?"

"Dinner is nothing, the tip of the iceberg."

"That sounds a little chauvinistic."

"It wasn't meant to be. I just think dinner at this nice quiet restaurant in Paris is where I will take you."

"Yeah, right!"

"That's not a pick-up line," Damian told her looking very serious as if it really wasn't. "Is Paris too short notice for you, because I'll accept your favorite restaurant, on me of course?"

Daniella thought about it for a few moments, and then nodded. "Sure, why not, Mr. Dame, here's my personal card, call me," she said as she handed him the card. "Nice meeting you," she sexily smiled before walking away.

Damian couldn't take his eyes off her backside. "The pleasure was all mine," he mumbled to himself.

Chapter Eight

The caravan of obsidian black Lexus LS 460L's turned the corner and pulled up to the massive cathedral. The first two men out of the cars jogged up the steep steps towards the chapel entrance, pulling out their silenced weapons half way up the stairs. The men who were standing outside of the church couldn't react in time. In one smooth motion, the men from the Lexus fired several silenced shots into each of them, and in one smooth motion, caught their bodies as they fell toward them. The bodies were handed off to other men from the cars, who waited patiently for the first two men to clear the rest of the cathedral. The first two men entered into the chapel doors, found their targets, and quickly placed more silenced rounds into the bodyguards. They caught their bodies before they hit the ground as well. Two more dark suited men entered into the cathedral, walked up to two more bodyguards, who were sitting in the church pews with their heads lowered, and placed silenced

41

rounds behind their ears. The guards never knew what hit them.

Dante Reigns walked into the cathedral, knelt, made the sign of the cross, and then proceeded up the aisle toward his target.

Don Graziella Biaggio was kneeling in front of the altar, engaged in silent prayer. He loved this time of day, where he could have peace and solitude, and engage in relaxing prayer. He had been paying the arch bishop for the last ten years to open up the church for him, so that he could have it all to himself during this time of the day. It was much more beautiful, and so much more sanctified, without the screaming babies, and irritable children echoing throughout its halls. This was the way for one to truly have his prayers reached by the blessed saints.

Don Biaggio made the sign of the crucifix across his body, kissed his fingers, and then rose from his knees. He turned, only to find Dante Reigns standing behind him.

"Dante!" the Don stammered. "What are you doing here?"

Dante smiled, and turned his palms up toward the sky. "We're at war, remember? I tried to explain to you and the others that it wasn't us that killed your associates, but you wouldn't hear it. No, you wanted blood. You sanctioned the hit on me, and your men carried it out, with my pregnant wife in the car with me. So now, here we are."

The don turned toward his men who were hunched over in the pews. Blood was pouring from the side of their necks. "What are you doing here? This is my church!"

"I'm here, bringing the war to you, just like you brought it to me," Dante told him. He held out his gloved hand, and one of his men put a silenced pistol in it. "Good-bye Graziella Biaggio."

"Wait!" the don shouted, holding up his hand. "Let me pay you! It was all... a misunderstanding."

Dante shook his head. "There was no misunderstanding. Damian's father-in-law did something very stupid. We told you that we had nothing to do with it. You didn't believe us, and you called for a war. You hit me with my wife in the car." Dante paused for a few seconds. "Funny thing about you fat Sicilian motherfuckers, as long as you ain't doing none of the dying, you're all for shouting war."

"You cannot do this!" Don Graziella Biaggio shouted.

"Why not?" Dante asked with a smile.

"Because this is a house of God!" the don shouted.

"Good," Dante nodded. "That means you won't have too far to travel."

Dante squeezed the trigger several times, sending the don flying back into the alter. They left his body lying sprawled out on the floor, with his blood running down the steps of the sacristy.

Dante walked into the hospital room where his wife was lying in a bed, surrounded by a forest of monitors and intra-venous drip machines. Halfway into the room he paused, stared at her, and watched her breathing monitor. Angela had an oxygen mask over her face, and she was connected to a ventilator, to assist her.

Dante pulled a chair up next to the hospital bed, and seated himself.

"Looking good, kiddo. You're hanging in there," he said as he rubbed her forehead and kissed her. Here, your hair is a little out of place. Let me comb it for you. I'll be sure to get a beautician in here tomorrow. Actually, I'll make sure that a beautician visits you first thing in the morning every day and we'll get your hair and nails taken care of."

The silence in the room amplified the sound of the pumps from the breathing machine.

"The doctor said that we're going to have a baby.

Angela, I am so excited. The family is happy. Everyone is really looking forward to the new baby." He paused for a moment. "So, what do you want, a boy or a girl?"

He looked around the empty room for a split second as if waiting for her to respond.

"No, it's a boy," he stopped talking to her for a moment, his wheels turning in motion. "Wait a minute...our trip...it's only a few months away. He sat in the emptiness of the room and stared blankly at his wife's motionless face.

Angela had planned a trip around the world by private jet, of course. It would be just the two of them and their first stop, Easter Island, Chile. Their *exploration* as he remembered her calling it would begin at Ahu Tongariki, a magnificent platform holding a row of fifteen enormous *moai*, a lavish barbecue picnic lunch at Anakena, where they'd spend the afternoon, playing on the beach and snorkeling in the water. Their next day would be spent traveling to Rano Kau volcano to see its vast freshwater crater lake and then hiking to some of the island's caves and continuing to mountain-top Orongo, once the center of the island's mysterious Birdman cult and visit Ahu Akahanga which legend says holds the tomb of the island's first king. After, two days, they'd be off in their private jet to to Apia, Samoa, Angela's favorite place on earth to sun bathe nude, and experience the most sensuous body treatments on earth. After a few hours of body rituals that would leave them glowing from the Polynesian sun, they'd embark upon Sydney, Austrailia. The penthouse suite in the Four Seasons Hotel, offered amazing views of Sydney's harbor and famous Opera House. Being their first time in Sydney, Angela planned to explore the historic Rocks District, into Paddington with its celebrated open-air market, and visit Bondi Beach. She had even planned a private $400,000 a week vessel to cruise her and Dante to a nearby island for an Aussie style lunch, just lunch. Sydney had an amazing Taronga Park Zoo with unique wildlife including wallabies and wombats so she added the zoo to the itinerary. After Australia and breezing through the down under, they'd be off again, to Bangkok, Thailand. She had reservations for dinner at The Oriental Bangkok, not far from their hotel, the Rambagh Palace. The next day, a private showing had been arranged for Dante and Angela to examine gemstones and Dante already knew that she'd *bond* with one if not two precious gemstones. Then, the following evening they would be privately jetting to Jaipur known as India's 'pink city' because of the magical glow that its famous pink stucco buildings emanate at night. A traditional Rajput warrior welcome with garlands and a tikka ceremony would be held in their honor as guests. The next day they would explore Jaipur and tour the ancient Amber Fort with massive ramparts, towers and domes surrounding a glittering chamber of mirrors. After lunch, they would continue to the City Palace Museum in the heart of the old city, Jantar Mantar observatory and the Palace of the Winds, with its honeycombed sandstone windows. And maybe squeeze in an unforgettable match of Jaipur elephant polo and of course, being so close, Angela chartered a short flight to Agra to see the renowned Taj Mahal, monument to love. Afterwards, they'd reboard the jet for Dubai. Destination, the Madinat Jumeirah, The Arabian Resort. Two days later, the plan is to depart Dubai for Cairo. Everything was on list and they would visit the Giza Plateau to see the Pyramids and the Sphinx. In Cairo, there were world famous Egyptian museums, the real life treasures found in the tomb of the boy-king Tutankhamun and Mummy Room, which houses the remains of 27 of his New Kingdom relations. The Citadel of Slah El Din, high above the city, and walk down from Bab El Fotouh into the heart of old walled Cairo and the Khan El Khalili Bazaar. She signed them up for a Camel caravan to ride them into the desert on the Giza plateau. And they'd enjoy Arabian night dinners in romantic Arabian style. Her last and final stop around the world was Seville in Spain, the magical capital of Andalusia. A city filled with history dating back to Neolithic times. They would occupy the penthouse suite in the Hotel Alfonzo XIII. And do nothing but sightsee the 14th century Alcazar, Europe's oldest royal palace still in use with massive famous gardens. There was the labyrinth traffic free streets of the Barrio Santa Cruz, the Gothic Cathedral, Casa Robles, Andalusia's finest restaurant, the Maria Luisa Park, the Plaza de Espana, and the Casa de Pilatos all on her list of places to visit. And for Dante, a visit to the most famous bull breeding farms in Spain, the Cortijo los Arenales, home of the Condes de la Maza. Dante sat back in his chair thinking about the day she came to him with the idea.

"Seriously, I can't just hop on a private jet and leave the family business for a month. Are you thinking of what you're asking, because Princess would completely take over and Damian, God only knows what would become of him."

"I know what I'm asking, I'm asking for my husband to do his wife, just the two of us, on a private jet, out there in the middle of world. I want to see the world before I get too old, I want to enjoy my husband's massive wealth and I want us to take lots and lots of pictures so one day we can show our kids that their parents traveled the world."

"You've already been around the world before."

"Yes, but I didn't go to these locations and neither have you, please say yes," she said as she put her arms around her husband and kissed his lips gently, "please, Dante, do it for me," she said.

"And what do I get for all this, Angela, what's in it for me?" he asked squinting his eyes at her waiting for an answer.

Angela bent over and began to whisper in his ear.

"Book it, book it now," he said as he began to kiss her and pull at her clothing. "What was that again about the camel and the desert, babe? Can you run that by me one more time?" he asked as she pulled his body down on top of her and wrapped her long, silky legs around him.

"I love you," he said as he bent down and kissed Angela, the beeping of the tubes that she was plugged into echoed in his head. "For what they have done...I won't rest...I will kill them all...for you, all for you."

Chapter Nine

"Happy Birthday, Cheyenne!"

The Reigns family was all gathered around the enormous outdoor table, wrapping up the happy birthday song. Dajon lifted his daughter over the birthday cake, so she could blow out the candles."

"Hold on, swallow first," Dante told her. "I don't want any candle spit on my piece of the cake."

"Uncle Dante!" Cheyenne cried out, laughing at her uncle. She took a deep breath, and blew out her candles. The family clapped and cheered.

"Happy Birthday, little girl," said Princess as she bent down and kissed her niece's cheek.

Anjouinette took Cheyenne's tiny hand and held a knife inside it, and helped her cut her birthday cake.

"First slice goes to the birthday girl," Princess declared.

Anjouinette passed out slices of birthday cake, while Princess and Mina passed out scoops of ice cream. Dante turned, and walked over to where his mother was seated under a canopy tent.

"I miss her," Emory told her son. "How is she doing?"

"She's...I miss her, mom."

"I know son, I know you do. The amazing thing about it is that even with her circumstances, she's giving you the gift of life."

"She's the most amazing woman I have ever known."

"Yes, she's quite a catch for you. I take my hat off to Angela. She's a fine woman to have conquered your heart. That there is not an easy thing to do, wouldn't you agree, son," his mother joked. "I wonder did she know she was pregnant?"

Dante thought about the night of the accident. How they were rushing to get to Damian's Bio One gala event. How he watched her dancing with Damian and how she said she wasn't feeling quite well.

"I don't think she knew," he responded unsurely. "No, I don't think she knew she was pregnant at all."

"Wow, son, a baby, isn't that something."

"Yeah, it's really something."

"I just wish she'd come back to me. I don't know what I'll do without her. She is my soul mate," said Dante feeling all was lost.

"Come, take a walk with me."

Dante followed his mother, by her side as she took his hand into hers. The smell of gardenia filled the air as they passed the flower beds and walked inside the house, down a long corridor, to the left and third door down into the study.

"I know you don't believe, but I do. God is here, he's with us right now."

"Mother, please, not God," said Dante never calling Emory mother, first off. And secondly, he had just murdered a man in cold blood inside God's house with no absolute remorse. Regardless of whether he was right or wrong, he couldn't call on favors from God, not now.

"Listen son, God knows war, God knows everything.

Have no shame, Dante. Ask him to bring back Angela and ask him for the wit and strength you will need to conquer all that you must do. He works miracles and if Davidian was here, he would tell you the same. This is where you're father would sit, study, and for the most part and in his own way, this is where he would pray."

Emory Reigns closed the door to the study, leaving Dante alone with his thoughts. Dante walked around his father's old cherry maple desk and seated himself in Davidian's overstuffed leather chair. He closed his eyes, clasped his hands together, and began to pray.

"I'm not too good at this," Dante started off. "I don't know what to say, or even how to go about saying it. I... I just know that I want my wife back and if you can bring her back to me then I really would like you to do that. I also need you to help me execute my plan. I am at war, but you already know that, and you already know that my plan is to kill my enemy. Help me God, help me kill them all. Show them no mercy and through you, give me your power, so I will annihilate them all...for Angela."

Chapter Ten

Damian walked through the pristine halls of Bio One until he reached the cafeteria. The Bio One cafeteria was a massive, thoroughly modern affair. It resembled a gigantic, white, pristine cafeteria, with futuristic seating and accoutrements. The food on the serving line and in the buffet was all you can eat. There was also a chain of food outlets lining a cul de sac past the cafeteria. Well known fast food-chains such as Cinnabon, Starbucks, McDonalds, Chick-fil-a, and Taco Bell. The six thousand Bio One workers had a wide variety to choose from.

Damian grabbed a chicken sandwich from Chick-fil-a, a bottled water and then headed for his usual table in the corner. He spotted her midway through the cafeteria.

"Daniella?" Damian called out. "Daniella!"

Daniella spotted Damian and rose from her seat. She knew that she had a stalker on her hands. "What are you doing here?"

"Just checking up on things," he answered nonchalantly wondering the same from her.

"Just checking up on things?" Daniella asked, lifting an inquisitive eyebrow.

"Yeah," Damian nodded. "I like to get in here and see how things are going. What are you doing here?"

Daniella smiled. "I work here. I'm a molecular biologist."

"You work here?"

"You seem surprised," Daniella smiled.

"You said that you had a Ph.D, but not in biology."

"I have an MD and a Ph.D," Daniella told him. "Is that a problem? You're not intimidated by educated women, are you, Dame?"

"Not at all. In fact, I wouldn't have it any other way."

"And now it's your turn to tell me what you're doing here."

Damian lifted his arms and spun around. "I own the place."

Daniella laughed at him. "Yeah, sure you do."

Damian extended his hand. "Allow me to introduce myself properly. My name is Damian Reigns."

Daniella's expression and demeanor quickly changed. She was talking to the owner of a megalithic corporation, who just so happened to be one of the richest men on the planet, who also just so happened to be her boss. She quickly played over their previous conversation in her head, hoping that she hadn't said anything offensive or stupid.

"What's the matter?" Damian asked with a smile. "You're not intimidated by educated, wealthy, powerful, men are you, Dan?"

Daniella laughed. He had reversed it on her.

"Why is it that this is the first time I'm seeing you here, Mr. Reigns?"

"Ah-un, the name is still Dame," he told her. "Don't go changing up on me, just because you know who I am now. Deal?"

"Daniella nodded. "Deal."

"The reason we probably haven't ran into one another, is because I usually come around on the weekends and check things out. But, I have a wedding to go to."

"I love weddings," Daniella said dreamy voiced. "Are you getting married?" she asked praying he wasn't.

"Umm, no, an old friend of mine from college. Would you like to go with me, being as though you like weddings and all? I need a date," he posed the question as if no was not an option and even more so as if his wife wasn't going to be there.

"Are you asking me out on a date?"

"Maybe, will you attend?"

"Maybe."

Now it was Damian's turn to laugh. "I was just about to sit down for lunch. Will you join me?"

"Well, I was just about to get back to the lab...I do have work to do."

"Trust me, it'll be okay if you're a little late getting back."

"And how do you know that?" Daniella smiled.

"Because I just so happen to know the owner of the company," Damian told her. He extended his arm.

"Oh, do you now?" Daniella took his arm.

"Yes, I do. He's really a swell guy," Damian joked about himself. "He's handsome, debonair and very intelligent. You can't help but to love him."

Daniella threw her head back in laughter, as they seated themselves at his usual table.

Chapter Eleven

Dante walked into the hospital room followed by a man wearing a white doctor's overcoat and a large identity tag badge.

"Mr. Reigns, how are you?" Dr. Michael Bailey asked shaking Dante's hand.

"I'm fine, Dr. Bailey," Dante told him. "How are you today?"

"Good," Bailey nodded. "Glad you're here. I wanted to talk with you about your wife."

"What about? Is there any improvement?" Dante asked.

Dr. Bailey peered at the other gentlemen in the room, wondering if Dante wanted him to speak freely.

"Oh, I'm sorry," Dante told him. "Dr. Bailey, this is Dr. Richard Holland, of The Bio One Memorial Hospital. He is a neurologist specializing in blunt head trauma."

Dr. Bailey exchanged a handshake with his colleague.

"You can speak freely in front of him, doctor," Dante

told him. "In fact, I would appreciate it if you would brief him in detail about my wife. Dr. Holland will be the lead physician treating my wife going forward."

"Oh," Dr. Bailey's voice reflected his disappointment.

"No offense, doc, you've done a stand up job," Dante told him. "It's just that he is one of the doctors from the hospital that my family owns and the interest there is intense as well as the various studies Dr. Holland has been conducting. And while they haven't been tried on humans, I want them to be tried on Angela."

Dr. Bailey nodded. "I understand. But I do have a question for you. Will you be transferring her to the Bio One Medical ?"

"No," Dante told him. "Dr. Holland doesn't want her moved, not even air lifted. So, we have no choice but to keep her here to keep her stable."

"Every precaution will be used to safe guard the unborn child," said Dr. Holland igniting the conversation.

Dr. Bailey pulled out a pen light, lifted one of Angela's eyelids, and examined her.

"She's completely unresponsive," Bailey told them. "I'm afraid that at this point, the only thing that is keeping her alive is the ventilator. I've scheduled her for several tests in the coming weeks. The MRI test will be the one that will tell us where we need to go from here."

"Bio One has an advancement radio wave neurometer?" Dr. Holland advised.

"A radio wave neurometer?" Dr. Bailey asked. "What's that?"

"State of the art imaging machine," Dr. Holland explained. "Like an MRI machine hooked to a supercomputer."

"I've never heard of one of those," Bailey told them.

"You wouldn't have," Holland told him. "There's only one in existence in the entire world. Bio One has it and I invented it."

"We should get the machine over here as soon as possible," Dr. Holland suggested. "There's no telling when she'll be stable enough to move safely."

"I'll have it here tomorrow if you need it," Damian said from the doorway.

Everyone turned in the direction from which the voice came.

"Damian, glad to see you," Dante said with a smile of relief. "They were just beginning to speak nerd. I need for you to translate."

Damian laughed and patted Dante on his shoulder.

"Anything you gentlemen need, you have it. The resources of Bio One are at your disposal."

"I want you to do everything possible, to save Angela," Dante said to both the doctors.

Dante turned and walked out of the room, followed by Damian. The hallway was filled with bodyguards standing post every ten yards.

"So, how is she?" Damian asked.

"Not good."

"Don't worry, Rich is the best in his field and his technology is superior. I wouldn't have sent him if I didn't think he could make a difference. He's the best in the country," Damian told him. "He'll get the job done. Watch him bring her back and watch that she'll be fine. The old Angela we all know and love."

"So, besides seeing your sister-in-law, what brings you here?" Dante asked.

"I wanted you to meet me at Southern Blues, but you didn't answer your phone."

"I was here, with Ange."

"Well, we need to talk, now."

"Let's go for a walk."

The two brothers began to walk the hospital floor, an

entire team of security detail beside them.

"The word is that the Old Ones have called for an army of soldiers from Sicily."

"So," said Dante, shrugging his shoulders. "They can call the Pope for all I care, I will kill each and every one of them and I will not stop until they are dead."

"I know but it is time, time to cut our ties with the Commission. Bio One is in place and in line and we will be in complete control of the entire pharmaceutical market once the RD package is approved."

"I hope it works for you, Dame. I do. But, right now, all I want is to get Angela back and I want them to pay for what they have done to her."

Damian looked down at his phone.

"I understand. We'll talk later. Just be careful and I've beefed up security, just so you know."

"Oh yeah...your new girlfriend?"

"My new girlfriend?"

"She checks out," Dante told him. She's legit."

"Good news, excellent news," smiled Damian, feeling the 'it' in romance budding uncontrollably.

"I checked her out personally," Dante reassured him. "Somebody has to look out for you."

"I just wish I knew what to do with Illyassa without causing more drama for this family."

"Her father will slice you in so many pieces I won't be able to find all your body parts. And Damian, I thank you for your misery."

"That's the first time, I ever heard you say that. I'd marry an old haggard woman and make love to her every hour of the day like she was the only woman walking the earth if it meant saving your life." Damian stopped, turned, shook his brother's hand, and then disappeared into the elevator.

"Thanks, Damian, I know you did that for my sake,"

said Dante in all solemnity. Then, just like the wind, a sudden change in his facial expression and back to ruthless. "Don't worry I have a plan for your dear, sweet wife." A nod of his head told Damian it was show time.

"Do I want to know?"

"Umm...no," Dante squinted his face, arched his eyebrows, smiled devilishly at his brother.

"Dante, I don't want her to be tortured or harmed," said Damian holding the elevator door.

"Would I do that?" he asked laughing as Damian stared back at him looking like a lost child from a third world, the elevator doors closing shut.

Don Crencenzo picked up the phone. The entire day had been spent on the phone with the Biaggio family and the death of Graziella. The Old Ones were in an uproar; Don Graziella Biaggio was one of the oldest and most respected dons, his father still alive, still living in Sicily, called for blood and revenge. He would have it too, for the life of Graziella one way or another.

Don Crencenzo hung up the phone, then immediately tried dialing the number again. Funny, the line seemed dead. He picked up the phone again.

"It's your security system Anastasio, it's tied into the phone lines," smiled Princess as she strutted across the dons office inside his private mansion.

"But, how, how could you get in here."

"I know it's built like Ft. Knox right? Well, that's what happens when your own security detail is for sale and can be bought to the highest bidder," she said as she sat down and crossed her long, toned legs, waving a Christian Louboutin heel in the air.

"This is insane," said Don Crencenzo as he tried pressing an emergency buzzer that sat on his desk.

"No what's insane is that you and your cronies

thought that you could just decide to start a war with my family."

"You started the war when you killed Marcellino, Gianpaulo, and Nicostrato."

"My family had nothing to do with their deaths and you know it. They were at the hands of Minister Malaika and yet you still came after us. Welcome to the party pal."

The silencer toned down the roar of the blast as bullets hit his chest one after another from the automatic weapon. Don Anastasio's body was thrown against the wall behind his desk before it slumped to the floor. Princess walked over to him and shot him once in the head, making sure he was dead.

Chapter Twelve

Grace Moore stood on the lawn of Reigns family ranch looking as if she had crawled through an underground tunnel in waist high 'God only knows what'. How she had managed to surpass surveillance cameras, high-tech security instruments and an army of security guards was beyond the imagination.

"Where is my son, Damian you fucking body snatcher?" she screamed at the top of her lungs. Over and over and over again, she could be heard screaming through the courtyard.

"Oh God, what is that noise," mumbled Princess as she rolled over in her sleep, adjusting her eye lid cover, yearning for the comfort of her penthouse and the orderly function her household provided her.

Dante stumbled out of the bed to witness Damian running across the Reigns family ranch lawn as he tackled Grace to the ground.

"Get off of me, where is my son, Damian?" she said as she began smacking him in the head, throwing jabs at his body, ready to stand off and straight karate chop him.

"Don't let her hit you like that, bro!" hollered Dante from his balcony over looking the lawn.

"Shut up Dante before I place your ass under arrest

and throw you in Guantanemo Bay where the fuck you belong," growled Grace as she looked up at him, as Damian wrestled her arms behind her back. Grace somehow managed to get her leg between his and without warning she flipped him over on his back, before karate chopping his chest.

"Oooh!" said Dante feeling his pain. "You shouldn't talk to me like that Grace. I'm not very partial to FBI agents, especially this early in the morning."

"Where's my son, Damian?"

"What is that God awful smell?" he asked looking at the mud matter now smeared all over his Versace sleep wear.

"Your sewage," spat Grace as if climbing through sewage drains was a normal morning routine for any mother looking for her young.

"You are a fucking nut case, you know that, right?" asked Damian completely disgusted and ready to shower.

"Just tell me where he is," said Grace, ready to body drop him again.

"He's in the house, slee..." before Damian could say another word, Damian, Jr., came running from the house, a big smile on his face.

"Mom, mom, what are you doing here?" he yelled across the lawn as he breezed by his father and ran into his mother's arms.

Their reunion was long over due. Grace had been on missions assigned to her by the government for quite some time. Not realizing the dilemma Minister Malaika had put the Reigns family in, she thought Damian had moved and was trying to keep their son from her as he had done in the past.

"Seriously, this is all just one big misunderstanding. I tried to call you, but your voice mail was full. Seriously, we'll be going back home soon."

"I don't want my son in danger. If he's in danger, you might as well let him come with me. I don't understand you at all."

The two of them continued their argument in front of their son. The bottom line was Grace could hoop and holler until the cows came home, Damian, Jr., would be going no where with her, today or any other day. He was property of the Reigns' and he would live with his father.

"Grace, I've told you before, if you want to be close to him, you are more than welcome to..."

"Don't fucking give me that, sorry son," she did stop in mid sentence to apologize for her French. "There's no way I'm living with you, under your roof and under your watch."

"Well, Grace, must we have this conversation first thing in the morning, in front of Damian?" asked his father.

"Yeah, mom, don't fight, I'm just glad you're here. What's that smell?" Damian Jr., asked before figuring it was his mom.

"You crawled through the sewage drains to get to me, mom?" he asked.

"It's the only place your father didn't have security, son."

"Wow, cool, mom, really cool," said Damian Jr.

"I'll be taking care of that immediately, you do know that right, you won't get in through the sewage next time."

"Oh, yes I will. Don't be a fool and think otherwise," smiled Grace as they all walked inside.

"You want to take a shower with me?" Damian whispered in Grace's ear.

Grace stopped dead in her tracks. "Have you lost your mind? Get away from me, Damian. Just get away."

It was a little past ten in the morning, the day just beginning. Salvatore Tiziano limped into the room where the 'big' machine was waiting for him. He absolutely hated this shit. He hated it all of it, especially the machines. The hospital itself was frightening enough, especially at his age.

62

The damn thing was almost like that commercial about the roach motels, you check in, but you don't check out. And he had a bunch of friends who checked in, but didn't get to check out. Now, it seemed like his number had been called. Only thing, he wasn't quite ready to go, not yet anyways.

The Don was grateful for his old age, but some days, like today, he wished that God would just smack the shit out of him and get it all over with. His gout was bothering him, his left hand was cramping from his arthritis, and his diabetes had him pissing like a race horse and now this, the big C.

Cancer was sirens song at his age. It was like God was yelling 'last call for alcohol'. Few at his age could survive the big C, the damn chemo therapy, the radiation treatments, the operations. It was tough to survive a fall, let alone a major surgery. But these were the cards he had been dealt. And so this was one more shitty hand he would have to play, in a lifetime filled with shitty hands. But he had always managed to make the best of them in the past. He had been a good earner; loyal, hardworking, stand-up. Never ratted anybody out, took his lumps like a man. He had worked his way up, stuck by his wife and his family, built himself from nothing, and provided a good life for his wife and children. Things hadn't turned out so bad. His Mariella, she had a happy life, God rest her soul. And the kids, little Nicky, Anthony, Dominick, Sal Jr., they were good kids. They had married good Sicilian women, gave him plenty of grandkids, and were all stand up guys. So yeah, all in all, he had done pretty darn good with the scraps he had been given. Now, all he had to do, was fight off this last monster, the Big C.

"Help me up on the table," the Don ordered his bodyguard.

"He'll have to step outside once we get ready," the nuclear med tech told him.

"Yeah, yeah, I know," the Don said, waving him off. "Tommy, go ahead and step outside. Matter a fact, go down and grab ya a magazine or something. This things gonna take a minute."

"Sure thing, Boss," Tommy told him. "I'll be right outside if ya need me."

The Don nodded and turned to the technician. "Is my ass showing? I hate these damn things. We can put a man on the moon, but we can't come up with a hospital gown that'll keep closed around my wrinkled ass."

The doctor smiled. "Mr. Tiziano, I'm going to inject you with some dye, so that we can get a better picture of what's going on inside, okay?"

"Why are you talking to me like I'm a three year old?"

"I just want you to be as comfortable as possible Mr. Tiziano."

"I guess I'm as comfortable as I'm going to get. Go ahead I'm waiting," he said ready for anything just wanting to get it all over with."

"Sure thing, Mr. Tiziano," the doctor said with a smile.

Salvatore Tiziano woke from his deep sleep with the whir of the motor from the bed sliding out of the MRI machine. Once out of the machine, he was handed his glasses, and a glass of water.

"You're going to be a little thirsty. Here, let me help you sit up, just take your time," he was told.

Don Tiziano gulped down the water and then put on his glasses. To his horror, Princess Reigns and her henchmen were standing around him.

"Tommy!" Don Tiziano shouted.

Princess seated herself on the edge of his bed.

"Tommy's dead, Sal, I'm so sorry he just can't answer you. Neither can Paulie, Richey and your driver. Nope, they're all dead my friend."

The Don closed his eyes and shook his head. "Just get it over with then."

"Oh no, that's not how this is going to work, no, no, no," Princess told him. "You're special so you have a special death. Of course you will die," she said unable to not laugh at him, "Just not today."

Princess rose from the bed. "You know you should always make sure the doctor treating you is your actual doctor. God, these hospitals are dreadful aren't there Tizi? God knows who can just walk right in off the street and inject you with anything. Isn't that something, you'd think they'd have more security in these places, wouldn't you?" she asked most sincerely.

"You're a sick, twisted bitch. You always were," said Salvatore.

"And what are you Sal, what the fuck are you? I'll tell you, you're full of radiological matter that I had injected into you. So, yeah, you're a dead man walking, but it's going to be a slow death, a slow and painful death. It's going to eat you alive from the inside, for the next two weeks. You're going to lose your hair, lose control of your bladder and bowl functions, you're going to vomit constantly, and your stomach is going to cramp so bad that you'll beg for death to come. I want you to suffer, like my nephew suffered, lying up in that hospital bed. I want you to suffer like my brother Dajon suffered, when he had to bury his wife. Did you really think that you could kill a Reigns and get away with it, you son-of-a-bitch?"

Don Tiziano leaned back in the bed defeated. All sense of hope had drained slowly from his body. And then he felt himself becoming sick. The Don bent over and vomited on the side of the bed.

"See, it's happening already, right in front of our eyes."

"Fuck you!" said the Don.

"You can't," she said laughing at him. "You can't."

She and her men turned and left the room.

Chapter Fourteen

Damian rushed through the halls of Bio One and took a flight of stairs down three levels to the 17th floor. A team of biologists and molecular specialists were in the room, the greatest discovery known to man had just taken place and standing behind the table, smiling ear to ear was Daniella. She looked as if she had just seen a ghost.

"Oh my God," she cried, tears of joy boiling in the corner of her eye.

"Congratulations, Dan, really you deserve it," a fellow white jacket said embracing her tightly.

"Oh my God, I can't believe it."

"I can you're such a genius. Do you know what this means, you'll be the most famous scientist in the world."

"And the richest," added Damian. "Is it true?" he asked uncertain of the news he'd been given.

"Yes, we have found a cure for the HIV virus, all stages, completely wiped out. The blood results just came back from the lab. It's wasn't just the formula that had been worked up, Daniella here altered the formula naming it RC-221."

"Where's your write up and intake?" asked Damian wanting to see if she had kept a log of all the scientific data, findings and conclusions so that the documentation could be recorded and followed again.

She handed him her log book, her eyes staring back into his. Her work was done. She could only imagine the size of the bonus check Damian would provide her. She had taken care of business and now she had every intention of pursuing Damian Reigns personally.

"Thank you, Daniella, thank you," said Damian Reigns, shaking her hand and congratulating her, as he hugged her tightly.

"Really, it was my pleasure," Daniella said as she looked in his eyes. "I worked day and night, I knew you wanted this. I knew that if Bio One found the cure to HIV, you'd be even more powerful than you already are. I did it for you, Damian."

Damian looked into Daniella's eyes and wanted to scream and jump for joy. That was how happy he was, that's how excited he was. Daniella had no idea how important she had just made herself to his life. Damian began messaging, e-mailing and texting his family and closest friends. Everyone who got his message was told there was a special celebration at Philippe Chows and to be there at 8:00 o'clock.

"Daniella, I'll see you at Philippe Chows," he said smiling from ear to ear.

"Yes, sir, whatever you say, boss," she joked giving him a soldier's salute.

"I can't begin to thank you."

"I'm sure if we put our heads together we can come up with something," she said demurely, daydreaming of taking back shots from him on a sandy beach under the Polynesian sun.

Chapter Fifteen

Dante Reigns stood patiently by the hospital bed as Dr. Holland examined his patient. Angela, now four months pregnant was coming along rather remarkably under the circumstances. The vitals of the baby were well, perfect for any fetus. Dr. Holland measured Angela's growing abdomen.

"Is everything all right?" Dante asked.

Dr. Holland nodded, "The baby is growing, and it appears that everything is just fine."

"That's great news!"

"What about Angela?"

"The same," Holland replied. "No change."

"But, don't look glum, Dante." He couldn't help but to hope for a small miracle. "I really believe that the treatments we will be using to stimulate various wave patterns to the brain will bring Angela out of her coma," Dr. Holland smiled giving Dante hope.

"You think your experiments will work?" Dante asked really wanting to believe.

"Yes, I do," Holland answered. "This is an unusual case. Dante, some patients come back within two weeks, that's usually the best, but, some...as long as twenty years and out of no where...poof! They wake up...I've seen it," he said convincing Dante to believe in what could not be explained. "I am very hopeful, Dante, very hopeful. Angela is fighting," Holland said as he patted Dante's back. "Her body is still trying to heal itself. The swelling in her brain has gone down. The baby is fine, healthy, and strong. She hasn't given up yet, so don't you give up on her."

Dante watched as Dr. Holland finished his evaluation. His mind traveled off to when he was younger and his college days at Princeton University, where he met Angela who was attending classes for her Doctrine in Sociology. He saw her coming out of Bob's, a local barbecue restaurant. Ignoring his own hunger, he followed her back to campus. She never once noticed. He couldn't help it, from the first moment he laid his eyes on her, he was hooked.

What is he looking at? She asked feeling her chest, looking down at her self, smoothing her hair. *He's so fucking handsome; I could do him all day on a Sunday.* He was walking straight towards her, his eyes piercing into hers.

"My name is Dante. What's yours?"

"What did you just say?" she retorted as if she didn't understand the English language, yet was speaking it.

"You heard me. I said my name is Dante. What's your's?"

She couldn't help but smile. "Are you bossing me or simply do not know how to address human beings," she spat back at him boldly playing hard to get.

Dante looked at her curiously. *So, she wants to play.* And with that thought, he turned and walked away leaving Angela completely confused.

"Did he just walk away from me?"

And everyday she looked for him. And everyday she was tormented that he was no where to be found. Until one sunny afternoon he crept behind her and asked her as if this was her last and final chance. "Are you ready to answer my question?"

She turned around and found him standing there as if

he were King of the Land and looked up into his eyes.

You walked away like a spoiled, rotten, baby looking for his mommy," she said laughing at him.

"You think that's funny?"

"Yes, yes I do?" she said as she watched him turn right around and walk away as he did the last time.

It wouldn't be until their third by chance meeting that they would formally become acquaintances.

"My name is Angela," she said as she raised her eyebrow at him, tired of searching the campus day and night for another chance encounter.

"Angela, that's it, Angela?"

"Yes, that's it, Angela?" she replied back.

"Well, about time, it's taken you what now, four months to tell me your name. I'm imagining sex could take a life time."

"Actually, today," she said turning and walking away.

"What time," he hollered in her direction.

"9:30, my dorm."

"What's your dorm number?" he asked.

"See if you can figure it out."

And of course Dante Reigns had it figured out before the day's end and was knocking at her door sharply at 9:30 p.m.

"Wow, crime dog look at you, you found me."

"Why wouldn't I?" he said arrogantly walking into her room and looking around.

"Well, good for you, I guess you win."

"Always, I always win, Angela."

"It wasn't that hard to figure out, all you had to do was ask someone. You act like you climbed a mountain to get here."

"Actually, I made a phone call and I had my private detail search you out here on campus. Did you know that there are thirteen girls attending Princeton with the same first name as you?"

She paused for a moment and looked at him oddly. "You're serious aren't you?" she asked.

"Look outside your window?" he said watching as she peeked out the blinds.

"Oh my God is that like your security?" she asked looking at the men in black suits with black glasses standing next to a Mercedes Benz 600S with black tinted windows. "Who are you?" she asked puzzled with confusion.

"I'm superman."

"Good, I always wanted to fuck a Marvel character."

"Superman isn't a Marvel character, you're thinking of Spiderman."

"Shut up," she said as she pressed her body against his, threw her arms around him and began kissing him passionately as if she had been waiting for him all her life.

"I've been waiting for you to find me?" she said as he pulled at her shirt revealing her left breast. "Ever since the first day I met you and you asked me..."

That was it, no more talking. Dante shut her up by putting his finger in her mouth for her to suck on, then unzipped his pants, and pushed Angela on her knees. She took his penis into her mouth and sucked him off as if he was the President of the free world and it was her official Monica Lewinsky duty. Dante would be hers, security detail, 600S and all. Before he could stop, he was holding the back of her head, ejaculating in her mouth.

"Fuck," Dante said letting her head go, feeling as if she had just sucked the life out of him. He began to feel weak, somewhat dizzy, and then he fell onto her bed, holding his penis in his hand.

"No, absolutely not, we're not fucking. You are a stranger. I think you should leave."

Is she serious?

"What do you mean, I'm a stranger. You just sucked

the shit out of my dick and now I'm a stranger," he said pointing to his penis still rock hard and standing at attention.

"There's no evidence of that," she said as she wiped the side of her mouth sounding just as cocky as him.

"You swallowed the evidence."

"True," she purred innocently.

"I'm a stranger? You're a nut case, a fucking loony tune. You do know that?"

"Call me Jessica Rabbit," she said laughing at him right before, he pulled her down on the bed.

"I said no, don't you know what 'no' means," she said as she punched the side of his body and tried to wrestle her self from him. He was strong way too strong for her, using his chest, he buried his body on top of hers, pinning her flat on her back as he used both his arms and hands to pull her sweatpants down to her thighs.

"Stop! Dante, I said no!"

"Shut the fuck up, you want it, you want it, stop playing games."

Before Angela could even fathom the obvious, Dante Reigns was inside her, fucking her, against her will, against her pleas. He did not stop, he was not gentle, and he covered her mouth leaving finger prints across her face so that she could not scream. He pulled at her Princeton Tiger tee shirt bearing her breast and began to suck on her, holding her face down with his hand covering her mouth.

Angela knew that technically in a court of law she was being raped, sexually forced against her will, pinned down, and outmatched by his strength. She lay still as he thrusted in and out of her. He was incredibly strong, incredibly well endowed and amazingly handsome and attractive. Technically, it was rape, but heart to heart it wasn't rape and she knew it. She was so hot and so wet, Dante slid right inside her, legs closed, pants half on. She wanted him to take her, she wanted him to force himself on her, she wanted the fight, she wanted to pretend she didn't like it, she wanted the fantasy, she wanted Noodles and she got him, the only difference was they weren't in the back seat of a car they were in her dorm room.

Dante reinvented Angela's entire sex life. He made her do things the average respectable girl would never do. She fed his vivacious sexual appetite realizing his was just as disturbed as hers. Public places, cameras, video tapes, and handcuffs were just the beginning. Dante and Angela took sex in the city and blew the town and if she hadn't been tied up a thousand times, his name wasn't Dante Reigns.

"Your pussy's mine, you hear me," he said whispering in her ear before he let her face go.

She said nothing to him that night, just silently watched him go. The next morning, two dozen, long-stemmed, red roses were waiting for her in her dorm with a note that read, *To Mine, From Yours.*

And that was the deal and it was set in stone. They stayed a couple for the next seven years. Broke up, got back together, continued off and on, but Angela was always the one, the only one whose mentality held him, challenged him, and matched him in every way. She wasn't pushy, wasn't insecure, and she never denied him and always gave him her full attention. Even when they weren't together, even when they would fall out and she'd scream, I hate you a thousand times, she would still be there for him.

He remembered when Damian first showed up with Jonel McNeal. He had fallen hard for little Miss FBI. But, Dante wasn't to be fooled. He saw completely through that Grace Moore FBI bitch the moment he laid eyes on her. Damian unfortunate for him, could not see past beauty. He'd follow a beautiful woman with a voluptuous body into Satan's den. Thank God for Angela.

74

"Angela!" Dante greeted the voice cheerfully. "How would your sexy tail like to go out for dinner?"

"Dante?"

"Yes, of course. Who else?"

The voice on the telephone exhaled heavily, and after a brief pause asked sharply, "What is it now, Dante?"

"Dinner, dinner and a movie."

"What do you really want?"

"I have someone I want you to meet," he told her. "In fact, you should already know her. She's an old classmate of yours from the university."

"Uh-huh," Angela suddenly caught on. "Well sure, Dante, dinner with you and an old friend, how could I resist? Besides, I know how you like to spend money and impress, and I stress lots of money."

"But of course," Dante smiled. "I know you wouldn't have it any other way, Angela."

"Good bye, Dante," she said sharply hating him for everything he had ever done to her in the past.

"Good...bye..." The line went dead before he could finish his sentence. Dante smiled at the fact that Angela still hated him, yet still couldn't deny him, ever in this life.

The dinner date went well, with Angela and Jonel exchanging college stories while Damian and Dante interposed with compliments, quick wit, and college stories of their own.

The boys escorted the ladies out of the restaurant into the cool evening air where they exchanged good-byes. Damian and Jonel quickly disappeared into the brisk, star-filled night, while Dante wrapped up his business with Angela.

"So?" he asked, as the tail lights from his brother's Ferrari faded into the darkness.

Angela turned toward Dante and allowed a smile to slide

across her gorgeous face.

"Well, for one, Livingston Hall is on Seventeenth and Jackson, not on Herman Street. Two, Jubilee Hall is off Meharry Boulevard, not Herman Street. Three, the library is on Seventeenth and Jackson, not Sixteenth Avenue, and finally, we wore white dresses during our induction ceremonies, not pink ones. Ms. Thang did not go to Fisk, has never set foot on a black college campus, and was definitely not raised in the South."

"Are you sure?"

"Dante, I'm a Southern belle, the only Georgia peach you've ever tasted in your life, trust me, we recognize our own. That bitch is from Iowa or Nebraska or from some lily-white place in the Midwest where they grow a lot of corn. Ask her about Huckleberry Fin; she might know something. But she damn sure doesn't know anything about the South. I bet she never has been to Georgia.

Dante folded his arms and shifted his weight to one side.

"And how do you know that?" he asked her.

"Listen to her voice, her speech patterns, darling. Historically black, she is not. Southern raised, not in this lifetime!"

"Angela, this is important. Are you sure?"

"Dante, I'm the best. I'm a speech pathologist, with a minor in sociology. And I went to Fisk, then got my Doctrine at Princeton, remember. If that bitch went to Fisk, then my father is Jefferson Davis. I don't think so!"

That was Angela, always on point, always there to rescue him. Dante smiled thinking of the battles and gun fights. They were a modern day Bonnie and Clyde. And she would always save the day.

"Okay, Dante, what mission requires me to wear this skimpy, two-piece, string bikini?" Angela asked placing her hands on her Halle Berry hips.

"I'll explain the mission parameters once we're out on the water," Dante told her.

Angela shifted her weight to one side, and folded her arms. "What mission requires that you have to tell me about it in the middle of Canyon Lake on a jet ski?"

"Angela, I just want to talk to you, okay? Can we just go out on the lake and talk?" Dante exhaled.

"Can't we talk here? Dante, you know how things are between us. Why do you want to go there?"

Dante frowned and shook his head. "Angela, you are one headstrong..."

"Bitch?" Angela unfolded her arms and placed her hand on her hips again. "Is that what you were going to call me? You seem to like that word when I don't bend to your will. You like calling me whatever you want, when I don't give in to you."

Dante lifted his hands. "Okay, okay, you win. I just thought I could talk to you."

Dante turned and walked to the lift mechanism. He slammed the lever forward, activating the hydraulic lift for the Jet Ski. The arm attached to the Bombardier jet ski lifted it out of the water again.

"Dante, what's the matter?"

"A lot."

Angela walked to where he stood. She placed her tiny, well-manicured hand on his cheek, and turned his face toward hers.

"This is important to you?"

Dante frowned and turned his head away. Angela reached around him and activated the hydraulic lift, lowering the jet ski back into the water.

Dante watched as she climbed onto the large, two-seat watercraft. Angela was as shapely as ever. She was built like a brick house, solid. She had enough ass to divide between three women, and it was all as solid as a rock. Her stomach was so flat and tight you could lay a marble on it and it would sit still. Angela wasn't runway model fine, she was raised in the south, cornbread-fed, whipped with a belt across the ass, American beauty fine. She could put on a potato sack and make it look provocative. Angela turned and peered over her shoulder at Dante.

"Are you coming?"

"I used to love it when you would ask me that."

Angela smiled. Dante climbed onto the jet ski and sat behind her. He placed the gun he held in his hand inside of the compartment just to the rear of the seat. Angela throttled up the engine and they sped off onto the lake.

"So, what's the matter, Dante?" she asked.

"Everything. We're having problems with everyone."

Angela peered over her shoulder, "Princess?"

"And the commission."

"What's going on with the commission?"

"They want Princess to replace Damian."

"What?" Angela throttled back and zigzagged to bring the jet ski to a stop. Once this was done, she turned and faced Dante. "Are they crazy? Are they suicidal now? Don't they know they'll be signing their own death warrant?"

"Well, actually, it's the boss who wants her in charge. He wants to unify his distribution network."

"It makes sense theoretically, but in reality, he loses power. With different states under different people's control, no one can become too powerful and he can play the heads of the organization off against one another."

"Like he's been doing."

"And, under one umbrella, the head of this unified network could just say fuck him and buy from someone else."

"Angela, I don't know what he's thinking."

Angela tossed her now wet hair over her shoulders. "And

the commission is backing their demise?"

"No, once it was exposed, they went wild."

"So why are they tripping with you?"

"Well, the meeting turned bad, and I had them thrown overboard..."

"Overboard?"

"The meeting was on Alemendez' yacht."

Angela laughed. She lifted her hand and caressed the side of Dante's face. "Dante, what am I going to do with you?"

Dante placed his hand over Angela's, and rubbed her hands. Their eyes locked. Angela turned away.

"Dante, let's not go there."

"I know," he lowered her hand from his cheek to his lips, where he kissed it. "I just wanted to talk."

"So, the family and the commission are at war. Once you recruit and call up all of your reserves, you're almost as strong as the entire commission united. You have more money, more political connections, a larger manpower base, and better generals. You'll win and El Jeffe has what he wants, a unified commission." Angela smiled, and caressed Dante's cheek again. "He started this war on purpose. He's forcing you to wipe out the commission and take over."

Dante grinned and stared off into the distance. "I didn't see that. Damn, woman, you're brilliant."

"Still brilliant," she told him with a smile. "Let me help you."

"How?"

"Give me an army, and I'll wipe out the commission. I'll solidify your hold on Louisiana, Oklahoma, New Mexico, and Arkansas. I'll take Mississippi, Arizona, Missouri, and Kansas. I'll make Emil one of your regional chiefs and then I'll crush Don Alemendez and give you all of Florida in time for your birthday. That will make you untouchable. El Jeffe will beg for your forgiveness."

79

Dante smiled. He knew that she was serious, and he knew that she could do it. He knew that she *would* do it. Angela had been his and Princess' top general. She had planned the family's wars and had personally taken Arkansas and Oklahoma, while he conquered Louisiana and New Mexico. She was Dante in a crimson red, two-piece string. Unfortunately, she left when the family drew down its army and changed directions. Dante would give anything to have her by his side again.

"No, Angela. I can't let you come back in that capacity."

"Or, if you like, I could take some men and smash Princess for you."

Dante shook his head. "I offered to send Emil one hundred men to help make Savannah part of his organization. I sent two hundred. I have another hundred laying low in Atlanta and a hundred men scattered throughout Florida, keeping an eye on Don Alemendez. Our boys in San Antonio, Houston, and Dallas have been given the order to recruit, and they've already gotten pretty big. I want you to organize, strategize, and conduct operations from here."

"Why not let me go into the field and conduct operations from there? It's more efficient, and besides, you know I'm a hands-on type of operator."

Dante shook his head. "You're too valuable to risk."

"Too valuable?" Angela recoiled. "Dante, this is me you're talking to. Besides, I'm an independent contractor, aligned with the family. I'm not one of your day-to-day people. Nothing will suffer if I catch a hot one."

Dante stared into Angela's eyes. "I will."

Angela frowned at first and then turned away. "No, Dante, let's not go there. You know better." She turned back toward him. "I thought we weren't going there."

"Angela, what happened between us?"

"Dante, you know what happened."

"Did you love me, Angela?"

"You asked me that in the past tense." Angela leaned back and rested her head against his shoulder. "Dante, I still love you, I never stopped. I don't think that I ever will stop loving you, but we can't go there, understand?"

Dante leaned forward and kissed Angela's neck. He followed that kiss with another and then one on her cheek. He made his way to her lips.

Angela turned her head. She stared into Dante's eyes and slowly, their faces drifted toward one another. Dante's tongue glided across Angela's tongue as they sat in the middle of the lake.

"Dante..." Angela whispered.

Dante quieted her by kissing her again.

Angela pulled away. She stood and turned around on the jet ski, and then reseated herself facing him. She climbed on top of Dante's lap and slid her string bikini to the side. Dante pulled his swimming shorts down and entered inside of her.

Angela moaned and wrapped her arms around Dante's neck, stuck her tongue inside his mouth, and began rolling her pelvic area in a forward thrusting motion. Dante closed his eyes, tilted his head back, and placed his hands on her thick, firm ass. He could feel her muscles contracting and expanding as she rode him.

"Dante, where's your gun?" Angela moaned.

"It's inside you," he replied.

"Dante, sweetie, unless you want to go before you cum, you'll get your gun," Angela continued her thrusting.

"Angela, what are you talking about?"

"I'm talking about three men on jet skis bearing down on us."

"What about them?"

"Men on jet skis don't wear black ski masks," Angela said still riding him.

Dante turned around and saw the men bearing down on

81

them. He grabbed his gun out of the compartment as Angela rose and turned around on the jet ski. She quickly started it, throttled it up to speed, and took off.

Dante and Angela sped into the recreation section of Canyon Lake. Other jet skiers, sailboats, large water trampolines, fishing boats, and tubers were spread throughout.

The ski masks kept coming.

"They're gaining on us!" Dante shouted.

"No shit!" Angela answered. "They have fast one-seaters and we're on a two-seat, waterborne pig!"

"You know what that means?" Dante shouted. He lifted his glock into the air and cocked it.

"It means, my Lord, that we are about to enter into an old fashioned joust."

Angela turned the jet ski around, skidding it across the water violently.

Dante shook his head and held on tightly to her waist. "No, Angela, that's not what it means!"

"Too late!" she brought the machine up to full throttle.

"Dammit!" Dante reached over her shoulder, aimed his weapon, and fired.

The jet ski rider in the middle flew backwards off of his machine. The other two masked gunmen returned fire. Two lines of water skirted by Angela and Dante's jet ski as they passed in between the two gunmen.

"Dammit, Angela! You don't play chicken with three guys with guns! Head for Damian's house!"

"Where in the fuck do you think I'm going?"

Dante peered over his shoulder. "They'll be catching up to us again in about a minute or two."

"Well, here's the plan. Once they get close enough, I'm cutting. That means the idiot on our right can't blast us without risking hitting his partner."

"And what if he doesn't give a shit about his partner?"

"Then we're all up shit's creek!"

The gunmen closed steadily and once they were within fifty yards of Dante and Angela, they opened fire.

Angela ducked her head.

"Shit!"

She turned the jet ski toward the left, bringing it across the path of one of the gunmen. Dante took aim and nailed the gunman on the right just as their jet ski collided with the gunman's on the left. The impact from the collision sent them all flying through the air. The jet skis themselves exploded into a fiery shower of fiberglass and metal. Pieces of the machines rained down on the area as Dante and Angela surfaced from beneath the water.

"Angela, are you alright?" Dante asked, as he swam toward her.

Angela nodded, as she doggie paddled toward the shore. Once she reached a shallow enough part of the lake, she stood and stumbled onto the shore, where she collapsed on the banks of the lake. Dante soon joined her.

"What happened to your plan?" he said, still holding the water-filled glock.

Angela sat up and stared at him. "You mean it didn't work?"

Angela broke out into a wild, uncontrolled frenzy of laughter. Dante quickly joined in. They laughed until they saw the gunman stumbling down the shore of the lake toward them. Dante lifted the weapon and pulled the trigger. The gun popped and the gunman fell.

"Dante! You should have taken him alive, so he could tell us who sent them."

"I know who sent them."

Angela looked in the direction of gunman, who lay on the ground holding his chest, and writhing in pain. "It could have been the commission or Princess or..."

"Angela," Dante interrupted, "Right now, they're all one and the same."

Dante smiled as he thought of the good old days, fighting with Princess for family reign and power. It's what they did, and Angela had always been there from the beginning, she was there. She was destined to be his wife. He remembered the day he proposed to her.

Bob's Barbecue was a small but popular mom-and-pop eatery located on the city's East Side. People from all over the country dropped by to sample Bob's tender, fall off the bone barbecue, smothered in his sweet, delectable, secret sauce. It was the envy of all other barbecue joints nationwide. It was this very same sauce that allowed the eatery to win award after award for its tasty barbecue. It was this very same sauce that brought Dante back, time after time.

Bob's was a friendly establishment, meaning it was in friendly territory, staffed by friendly people, most of whom the Reigns family had helped in some form or fashion along the way. It also meant that a heavy security detail was not necessary.

Dante entered into the small, smoky establishment and ventured to his left, where he took up his usual seat in the corner. His bodyguard, Greg took a seat in the corner, while another one of his bodyguards, Pete, went to secure the orders for the food. Pat and Melvin, two more members of his personal protective detail, ventured to the right, and took up a seating position across the room so that they could keep an eye on the front entrance. Ron, the fifth and final member of Dante's detail, stayed outside and watched the vehicles.

Car bombs had a way of finding their way underneath unoccupied vehicles sometimes.

Dante lifted his hand and peered at the diamond and

platinum Piaget watch wrapped around his wrist. He was busy thinking about how she was always late when she breezed in.

Angela spied Dante in his usual corner seat and headed for the table.

"Sorry, I'm late," she told him. She offered a friendly smile to Greg, who relocated himself to the table next to theirs.

"Don't worry, I'm used to it," Dante told her with a smile.

Angela plopped down in the chair directly across from Dante. She leaned to the side and sat a large Hermes Birkin handbag on the chair next to her. Pete brought them their food and drinks, placed them on their table, and walked to the far side of the room. He stood directly between Dante and the door.

Dante lifted his hand and motioned toward the white Styrofoam plates. "I hope you don't mind, I took the liberty of ordering for you."

"Thank you," Angela smiled. "I see that you still know what I like."

"Of course, how could I ever forget?"

Angela adjusted herself in her seat. "So, what's the deal, Dante?" She lifted a piece of smoked sausage and bit into it. "And give it to me straight, no bullshit."

"Always, so very ladylike," Dante smiled. "It's your timidity that has always attracted me."

Angela tilted her head and scowled, "Ha, ha, very funny. Look, time is money, and in my case, a lot of money. What's the assignment?"

"Marry me."

"Ha, ha, super funny. You're a regular comedian today." Angela lifted her styrofoam cup and sipped at her lemonade.

"Give me the job description and I'll give you my price."

Dante waved his hand and Greg stood. He dug inside of his dark gray jacket pocket and removed a small, black, felt box. He handed the box to Dante.

Dante sat the ring box on the table and then pushed it across the table to Angela.

"Open it," he told her.

"Dante, I don't have time for this." Angela lifted her petite hand and glanced at her wristwatch. "You want me to pose as your wife, that's fine. Just give me the parameters of the mission so I'll know what to wear, what to do, who to be, what voice to use, and everything else. I don't have time to play twenty questions or the guessing game."

"Dammit, Angela, if you'd just be quiet for a minute and listen, you'd understand that I want to marry you!"

"Marry me? You mean, marry me as in a wedding, a real wedding, one with tuxedos, sappy, pink bridesmaid dresses, and little, snot-nosed kids throwing flowers all over my shoes? Is that what you're asking?"

Dante nodded.

Angela Paxton broke out into an uncontrollable stream of laughter. "Get serious. You've got to be shitting me, Dante."

She rose from the table and bent down to grab her purse. Dante grabbed her hand.

"Angela, look, I'm serious. I...I made a mistake."

Angela rose and stared Dante in the eye. "You're goddamned right you made a mistake. Dante, how dare you! How dare you bring me here and propose to me! How dare you propose to me period! You had your chance Dante, remember?"

"Angela, I was a boy then!" Dante rose. "I was a childish, little boy with no idea of commitment. But now, now I'm a man, Angela. And I know what I want. I know what I need. There's nobody for me, Angela, nobody. Just you."

Angela exhaled loudly and shook her head. She sat back down at the table and stared at him.

"Dante, why now? What is all of this about?" Angela frowned at him. "Are you going to jail or something?"

Dante laughed. "No, I'm not going to jail. What this is

about is tying up all loose ends. It's about completion. It's about realizing my mistakes and trying to make them right. Angela, you're the only woman for me."

Angela frowned. "And why is that, Dante?"

"Because you won't take any of my shit."

Angela and Dante laughed. Dante nodded his head toward the ring.

"Open it," he told her.

Angela lifted the black, felt box and opened it. Inside sat a flawless, ten-carat round diamond, nestled on a six-prong, platinum base. Angela gasped and her hands rushed to her face, covering her mouth.

"Oh my God!" She looked up at him. "Dante, this is beautiful!"

Dante removed the ring from the box, took her hand into his, and then placed the ring on her finger.

"I should have married you back then, Angela. I'm sorry. I'll never let you go again."

Tears came to Angela's eyes. She stood and walked around the table to where Dante was standing. He wrapped his arms around her and hugged her tightly.

"I love you, Angela. I love you more than anything in this world. I want you," he whispered softly.

She looked up at him and smiled, "Dante, do you really mean that? Can you really say that you feel that way?"

Dante nodded.

Angela held her ring up to the light and examined it, "Oh, my God. This means that I'm going to be related to Princess!"

Dante laughed.

"Dante, I will beat that bitch's ass if she gets out of line at my wedding."

Dante laughed and hugged her again.

Angela pulled away from Dante and looked around the smoke filled establishment. "Uh-um, why in the hell did you bring me here to propose to me? Why couldn't I get proposed to at a fancy French restaurant or something? And what ever happened to the get down on one knee thing? Oh, you're going to pay for this."

"Angela, this is where we first met, remember?" Dante lifted his arms into the air. "This is where it all began. What better place to come full circle..." he asked as he spun around. It was then, he saw them.

Dante shoved Angela to the floor and went for his gun, "Angela, stay down!"

The two suited gentlemen in line with the other patrons turned and opened fire. Pat was struck in the forehead above his right eye, while Melvin took his bullet in the ear. Dante fired his forty-caliber glock and struck the first suit in the chest. The impact from Dante's bullet caused him to fly back into the crowd. The second suit ducked behind a wall.

The guy wiping the tables pulled from his apron a large chrome Smith and Wesson automatic, and put a nine-millimeter round through the back of Pete's head. He turned to fire at Dante, but was caught in the chest by a forty-caliber round from Greg's handgun. Angela crawled to her Hermes handbag and pulled from it her micro Uzi sub machine gun pistol.

From the rear of the restaurant, another suited gentleman stood and fired a Mossberg pump shotgun toward Dante and Greg. A large chunk of the wooden table disintegrated. The suited gentleman stepped from behind the wall and fired at Greg, catching him in the shoulder. Dante fired back, striking the wall just in front of him.

From the area near the rest room, three suits appeared. Angela let her Uzi pistol loose. It burped rapidly, spitting nine-millimeter rounds across the wall and across their chest. They fell instantly.

"They're all over the place!" Greg shouted. "We've got to get out of here!"

The shotgun came over the counter again, and Greg put a bullet through his forehead. Another suit quickly replaced the one who was firing the shotgun. This suit, however, held in his hand a Mac 10 submachine gun. He opened it up.

Bullets ripped across the wall just behind a ducking Dante and Greg, leaving a straight line of holes across the wall. The room was filled with smoke.

The suit hiding behind the wall stepped out and fired again, striking the table just next to Angela's head. Pieces of wood splintered off and struck her on her right cheek.

"Dammit!" she cried out. "These sonsofbitches are coming from everywhere. They're like roaches!"

The Mac 10 fired again, striking Greg in his shoulder, causing him to drop his gun and cry out. Angela sent a full barrage toward the suit with the sub machine gun. The suit slumped over the counter and his weapon fell from his hand.

The suit hiding behind the wall grabbed an old lady from off of the floor, and put the gun to her head. He started for the door using the old lady as a shield. Dante smiled.

Dante lifted his glock and pointed at the old lady, putting several shots in her. She fell, leaving the suit exposed. Dante smiled and then put a bullet through the suit's eye. He turned and grabbed Angela.

"Let's go!"

Angela pulled his arm. "Not the front door! Your driver's dead! We're going through the side door. My Porsche is parked on the side!"

Angela walked to the side door, and pointed her gun at it. She fired through the door, just in case someone was standing on the other side of it. She then shifted her aim and blew the locks off of the door. They raced to her car.

Greg climbed into the back of the 911, while Dante climbed into the passenger side. A suit stepped from around the rear of the building, and Dante stuck his gun out of the window and put a bullet through his heart. Angela hopped in the driver's seat, revved up her Porsche, and pulled off.

Dante turned toward her, "Welcome to the family."

"Princess?" Angela asked while breathing heavily.

Dante nodded.

"Can I kill her before the wedding or do I have to wait until after the wedding?"

Dante laughed.

Angela hit the highway.

Dante remembered that day like it was yesterday. He could never forget the day he proposed to Angela, the day she agreed to be his wife. She had been a part of his life for close to twenty years and she always would be. *I know you're going to be alright, I just know it.*

Chapter Sixteen

Minister Malaika was the Minister of Intelligence and Minister of the Secret State Security Service for the Federal Democratic Republic of Ethiopia. He was well respected and loved by the people of Ethiopia. Immanuel Hillel Malaika was believed to be the future president of his country and as such had great political and powerful friends across the globe.

The Minister sat on a throne imported from Sudan decorated in gold, rubies, emeralds and diamonds, worth many millions. For him the chair represented his greatness and his power. He lived a lavish, palatial life. There was no expense he spared for himself or his children. He looked at the picture of Daisalla sitting on his desk. His heart ached and mourned for her and he knew that until the La Costra Nostra was defeated and the Dons annihilated, Daisalla would have no peace.

His international contacts had been keeping him abreast of the Reigns family. So far he was pleased, very pleased with his son-in-law, Damian. However, his daughter Illyassa was of more concern, to say the very least. It seemed her flamboyant American lifestyle had taken a turn for the worse. If the reports were true, she would need to return back to Ethiopia immediately.

A security detail had been assembled to travel to Hollywood, California where Illyassa was staying. The Minister didn't understand her. All the comforts, amenities and everything she could want had been handed to her on a silver platter. Yet, even with all the persuading, she didn't want it. She said, "Daddy, please, I want to act so desperately. I want to walk the runways in Milan. Please father, please." And she did it. She made it. She had accomplished what some had said she could never. She was America's Top Model as if Tyra Banks had said so and she was racking in the dough. Her current contracts were with DiModolo, Versace, Louis Vuitton, and Creed. She had a casting call for the lead part in a new movie starring Denzel Washington and a chance encounter had pre-arranged for her to meet him later this evening. Illyassa looked at herself in her compact mirror and snapped it shut realizing there was not a single flaw in her reflection.

"Driver, please step on it. I can't be late," she said thinking of the last encounter she had with her lover. *God if Damian ever found out, he'd kill me.* Illyassa looked out the moving window thinking of Damian. *I should have never married him. He only married me for the sake of his stupid brother's freedom. I know he never loved me, he gets what he deserves.* She rationalized all this in her head, while picking her finger nails. She pulled out a small compact case and opened it up to reveal three grams of cocaine powder. *Thank God Los met me this morning. I have no idea how I'd get through the day.* She snorted the coke thinking of how she would fuck her lover all night long. Every chance there was to secretly meet, they did. Always the same place, the Beverly Hills Hotel, always the same bungalow, always in the garden, with a private entrance, a private butler, and just the two of them, just their little secret. The affair had been going on shortly after she married Damian. And who could blame her. Damian, was always working, always at Bio One, a mad scientist determined to save the world. She had no time for that. She was young, too young. She should have never married. Honestly, Damian wasn't enough man or maybe he was, just too busy a man to handle her needs, keep up with her night life, satisfy her libido.

Just then her cell phone rang from inside her oversized twenty five hundred dollar Louis Vuitton bag.

"Jesus, where is my phone?" she fussed at herself, snapped the compact case closed, reached in her bag, and fished around before her hands fumbled onto it. "Hello," she barked.

"Illyassa, hi, it's me Damian."

"Oh, you," she said rolling her eyes in her head.

"Guess what, I have the best news, you won't believe what has happened at Bio One."

"Ummm, let me guess, you lost your little guinea pigs and all those other rodents you've captured against their will so you could torture them with your concocted potions of only God knows what mold spores you've found off a dead yak's ass somewhere in the middle of a third world country?"

Why did I call her? Why do I even bother? I hate this bitch.

"Never mind, Illyassa, I'll call you back."

"Great, I'm running late for a meeting, toodles."

Did she just say toodles and hang up on me?

Just then Illyassa's phone rang again. In between snorts of cocaine, she answered.

"Yes, hello," she snapped as usual until realizing it was her only life line from who is a millionaire.

"Yes, daddy, I'm fine, she said fumbling her compact case of cocaine as it fell to the floor. "Daddy, please hold on." She reached down and grabbed the compact case, opened it, snorted one more time and then picked the phone back up.

"I'm sorry daddy, I couldn't hear you. What did you say?"

She heard the words, safety, and security detail and time to pack but he couldn't in a million years think that he could interfere with her acting career, not when she was on the brink of being discovered by Denzel.

Jesus he's insane.

"Daddy, now is just not a good time. I have an audition tomorrow and a very important meeting scheduled this evening. I just know that I'm going to get the part, daddy. I just know I am. Please daddy, I will be safe don't you worry. I love you and I'll talk to you soon, gotta go, daddy. Bye, daddy, love you," she said completely over talking him before hanging up the phone and refusing to answer him when he called her back.

The Minister listened to his little girl brushing him off as if he were some sort of servant being ushered away. *Who does she think she's talking to. I gave her an order.*

The Minister quickly dialed another number. A man answered on the third ring.

"Is the security detail ready for travel?"

"Yes, sir, everything is in place, sir."

"Go get my daughter from the dreaded Americas and bring her back her at once. And be careful with her."

Chapter Seventeen

The remaining dons all gathered at Bice in New York City. Sitting at a round table, Don Vincente Pancrazio, Don Tito Bonafacio, Don Luigi Gianchetta, and Don Carlo Cinzia were the last of the New York Old Ones left standing.

"God bless the dead," spoke Bonafacio, waving his glass in the air, toasting his lost brethren, Don Biaggio, Don Tiziano, Don Giovanneta, Don Constantino, Don Cipriano and Don Crencenzo.

"To made men," said Pancrazio.

"To Sicily," toasted Don Gianchetta.

The men drank Merlot and began eating, passing the plates of food amongst themselves.

"Everything is in motion. That fucking Ethiopian moulee won't know what hit him. By the week's end, the country will be appointing a new minister," declared Pancrazio.

"What about the Reigns?" asked Cinzia.

"Damian, Dante and that bitch sister of theirs are all on the list," answered Don Gianchetta. "The boys from Sicily know what to do. Don't worry they'll handle it," he continued, smiling at the happy thought of the demise of the Reigns family. "Everything they've put the families through, they deserve what they get," he said pounding his fist on the table.

"And the replacements?" asked Bonafacio, "When will they be appointed?"

"They are being made as we speak, I'm waiting on the phone calls, any day now and we'll know who'll be appointed and who'll be taking over the families," Don Pancrazio replied.

The dons had certainly been busy over the last few weeks. Sicily had inherited the debt of organizing the new dons thanks to Minister Malaika and the Reigns family. Everyone had beefed up protection and added more detail to their security teams. Their armies were strong and no stone was being left unturned when it came to protection. The Old Ones were smart. They had been around the longest, inherited Las Vegas and built it from the desert up. They owned and controlled Atlantic City and to list their territory would take all night. The mafia controlled it all, even parts of the government, their power was strong. From local law enforcement to federal FBI agents, judges, mayors, city unions and councilmen the mafia had their finger on everyone. Like a puppet master, they controlled the strings and they always won, always.

"Everything is in place and it's only a matter of time, for them all, just a matter of time," smiled Don Pancrazio.

Chapter Eighteen

Illyassa spread her legs as she lay back on the bed, she loved her secret escapades of sinful, deviate sex. She grabbed her breasts, squeezing them tightly together. Then, she let one hand go, grabbed the sheets beneath her ass, raising her torso as she received the most intense head ever in her life. It was like her body was in a rhythmic wave and she couldn't escape it.

"Don't stop, please, don't stop. Oh God, please. It feels so good, oh God. I can't take it, lick my pussy, oh it feels so good, yes, right there, right there," she said feeling her lover's tongue glide in and out of her. Unable to hold it any longer, Illyassa came, in waves before she rolled over and hugged the sheets as if they were holding her body in a sacred and safe place.

"I can't go on like this, I just can't. I can't live with this lie. Don't you think we should tell him?" she asked.

"Tell who?"

"My husband, your brother, who do you think?" she asked looking confused.

"I wouldn't think to tell my brother anything. Besides, don't you think he already knows about us, Illyassa? Please, what do you take Damian for, a fool?"

"What makes you say that? What makes you say he knows about us?"

"Because...you know, Illyassa, I would think that you would be a little bit more concerned about your father finding out about us, before you would care what Damian had to say," smiled Princess.

"My father? My father? What does he have to do with this conversation?"

"He is the only one you should be concerned with, Illyassa. I think he is the one that needs to know that you're filing for a divorce, don't you?" said Princess as she picked up a cigarette and lit it, while lying naked next to Illyassa.

"But, I'm not filing for divorce," Illyassa retorted.

"Yes, yes, yes, you are, first thing in the morning," she said as if reporting the Colbert Report on Comedy Central.

"What are you talking about Princess, you don't make any sense."

"I want you to call Damian tonight and tell him that you want a divorce. You can be nice to him and gently break his heart or you can be a bitch about it and tell him that you never loved him and you simply married him because you had nothing else better to do with yourself. Either way you will tell him tonight and you will file your paperwork first thing in the morning."

Illyassa sat up on the bed and looked at Princess as she inhaled on her nasty cigarette. *Who does this bitch think she's talking to. I am of royalty, she tells me nothing.*

"And what if I don't call Damian and do as you say."

"Illyassa, you don't want to know the answer to that. Really, you don't want to know, really, really," said Princess as she began to laugh at the mere thought of Illyassa. "I don't even want to spare you the details of what could happen. Really, I don't...," said Princess coming to an upright position before hopping off the bed. "But, if you insist, I will," said Princess as she began to pace across the floor in her birthday suit before sliding on her Guia La Bruna Summer Tale bra and thong. "See, Illyassa, this is how it works," she said bending over and leaning in on Illyassa. "Didn't you say you wanted to be an actress? Well, let's just say you've already debuted in your first feature film, not yet titled, but rated X," she smiled and then stood straight back. "And guess who'll have the best seat in the house when watching your performance?" she pretended to ponder, placing her finger on the side of her forehead. "Umm, let me see...your father, Minister Malaika. And he can watch you and with the help of the internet, so can the world, but first...daddy."

Princess stopped talking and watched Illyassa as she digested the bottom line. Quickly, her mind scrambled. All the nights they had shared. *It's no telling how many tapes she has of us together.* Illyassa got the point of how the situation could easily unfold, how bitterly hurt Minister Malaika would be, how she would cause their country shame and humiliation and how easily she could be disowned by her father and stripped of her title and her inheritance.

Princess could be heard in the distance explaining detail by detail of how her father would receive the package, open the package, find the tape, play it and then kneel over and die of a heart attack. Not to mention, how within 48 hours of him playing the tape, it would then air on You Tube. Isn't it rather genius," asked Princess.

"I fucking hate you."

"I wouldn't say mean things to me right now Illyassa, you never know whose listening. Shhh!" smiled Princess as she slipped on an Escada pant suit and clicked her heels into a tan pair of Monolos.

"What about Damian?"

"He's celebrating tonight, Illyassa, without you his wife, who doesn't care. You're holding him a hostage, but thank God I've freed him. You weren't that bad of a cunt to deal with. I actually enjoyed fucking you, even though you slept with my brother. God, Illyassa, make the call, you don't want daddy to find out what a coke whore his precious baby girl turned out to be," said Princess as she picked up her diamond and alligator Chanel handbag worth every bit of a quarter of a million dollars. She threw the diamond strap around her shoulder and walked toward the door.

"I hate you!!!" screamed Illyassa throwing the clock radio from the night stand at Princess as she walked out of the room and into the Hollywood sunset.

"No, you don't, you hate yourself," mumbled Princess closing the door behind her as she walked out of Bungalow 8.

Chapter Nineteen

Damian Reigns studied himself in the full length mirror as he smoothed his hands down his Kiton suit. He was standing in the middle of his walk-in closet facing the northern wall. The closet was actually two rooms, thirty by forty-five feet and was designed to hold all his clothes, shoes, coats and jewelry. To say the least the space was overcrowded to be so massive. He looked around his palatial estate, he missed his home. *I can't wait to move back in,* he sighed before flipping the switch and walking down the hall.

He had a fleet of automobiles in a showroom style garage. Tonight, he planned on pulling out the stops and his Ferrari 599 GTB Fiorano. The car had 620 horses and could do sixty miles per hour in three point seven seconds, and hit a top speed of two hundred and five without breaking a sweat. She was beyond sweet. The Ferrari actually belonged to Dante. One day, out of the blue, he said he didn't want the car anymore. Damian didn't even question him. Simply slid the keys out of his hand and brought the car home, parked it in his garage and drove it every now and then for fear Dante would want it back. The car really was a piece of work, with fifteen thousand dollar custom racing wheels and a custom Alpine white interior with dark blue piping, and a Blaupunkt sound system, who wouldn't love it. He grabbed a bottle of Voss from the frigidair inside his garage showroom. He felt like he was on top of the world. Everything he had worked so hard for was about to pay off. He couldn't imagine that in a million years he would hold in his hand the cure to anything, let alone the cure for AIDS. He thought of all those throughout the world infected by such a deadly disease. *Wait until the government gets these test studies,* he knew the battle would need to be politically strategic. Currently, the Food and Drug Administration had over forty eight different medications prescribed to people with the HIV virus. In the world of selling drugs, it was big business to say the least. If anything, Damian already knew that the government would do whatever they could to stop him. Forget the sick and all the people around the world that would die as a result, the bottom line was the government sold drugs. They were called prescriptions and just like any other drug dealer, they too depend on your sickness and they got just what you need. *We'll see what you do, but I'll help all the sick people I can.* He stopped for a moment and thought of RD-221 and RDX-214 which the FDA had yet to respond to. *They probably won't either. Why would they, my anecdotes will cure various forms of cancer and put them out of business.* If you asked Damian and Dante Reigns their personal opinion, the government made everybody sick so they could make millions and millions of dollars keeping everybody well. It was a well kept secret that there were cures to all types of diseases and viruses, but you had to go to other countries to receive treatment. *Well now no one has to go anywhere. I got the cure to AIDS and I'm going to make sure the world knows it.*

     Damian finished the bottle of VOSS and put the empty glass bottle in a recycle bin before clicking the door locks with his remote control key. He opened the door and sat in the passenger seat of the Ferrari. His nostrils inhaled the scent of imported Italian leather and he put the key in the ignition. He turned the key but the car didn't start, it made a whirring noise, but wouldn't turn over. He immediately jumped out. He picked up his phone and called the head of his security detail, which his cousin Brandon had arranged.

The phone rang two times before William picked up.

"My god damn car won't start. I don't know what's wrong with it," said Damian as he closed the car door and began to walk back inside the house.

"I'm going to have to go back inside and get the keys to my Rolls Royce. I'll be ri..." the explosion came with out warning and the thrust of the fire and air combustion blew Damian off the ground, propelled his body into the air, and crashed him into the side of a Rolls Royce coupe.

His security detail broke through the locked door from the outside and rushed into the garage show room. One of the guys all dressed in black, grabbed a fire extinguisher and began to spray the fire engulfing the Ferrari.

"Where is he, he's not in the car," said Pedros a henchmen assigned to protect Damian.

"Over there, look," said William, running to Damian's body lying lifeless by the side of the car.

"Call for an ambulance! Hurry, call them, quick!" said William as he felt for Damian's pulse. "Thank God, he's still alive!"

Chapter Twenty

Illyassa sunbathed thinking of her sordid affair with Princess. *That bitch will get hers one day.* Divorcing Damian was the last thing Illyassa was planning to do, or at least, it was the last thing she was planning to do in the near future. Truth was she loved being married to Damian. She loved everything about his power and his vast wealth. How else would she have escaped the compound her father called a palace? Not to mention, how in the world would she have been able to romp around the Americas her father certainly would have never stood for that, but having the stature Damian Reigns had, it was the absolute perfect union at the absolute perfect time. The wedding was a picture book fairy tale and Illyassa was the epitome of unsurpassed beauty. Any man would be a fool not to marry her. She was beautiful, wealthy and let's not forget that she came with her own army and more political connections than the Reigns family could imagine. Yet, four months after the honeymoon, she wanted to move to Hollywood to pursue her acting career. So, she purchased a seven thousand square foot mansion resting quite comfortably on Mulholland Drive. It was a mansion in the sky to say the least. For Damian, his life couldn't be more perfect, with him being the womanizer and playboy that he was, he was actually comfortable with the idea when she proposed the same one night while they ate dinner. He jumped on Air Reigns One and flew her out to Los Angeles the next day she barely had time to pack. It was complicated to say the least, but in short their union had sealed Dante's freedom. Illyassa's father called in favors for the sake of his newfound in-laws. In a way, Damian felt bad for her having sicked his evil sister on her, but what choice did he have. She had abandoned their marriage, technically abandoned him. And left him in a situation where he was forced to look over his shoulder for fear her father was silently watching him. It was Dante who put the bug in the air.

"Look at you? What do you think might possibly happen if your wife or her father finds out about you and these America's Next Top Models your romancing, huh brother? What do you have to say for yourself?"

"What can he do, he's in Ethiopia and she's living her life sleeping with every actor you can think of in my house on Mullholland Drive, fucking right in front of the security, I might add. Please, Dante her father better not find out about her indiscretions, how's that. She's a Fifty Cent mix tape for God sake! Can you even imagine?"

"Say whatever makes you feel better, but Damian, you're playing a very deadly game with these people and you need to fix this problem."

"Fix it how?"

"You're the fucking genius, you can figure out everything else. She's your wife, figure it out," said Dante stressing the word 'your' to his brother.

Damian looked up from his desk at his brother's face.

"I want to divorce her."

"It isn't going to be that simple, actually, I don't even think you could say the word without starting a war," said Dante before adding, "Think straight man."

"I know you're not telling me to think straight," said Damian as Dante shook his head pathetically at him.

If Damian were to be caught God forbid cheating on Illyassa and break her heart and a call be made, geez Louise,

Dante didn't even want the headache. He knew his brother, he knew him like the back of his own hand. And there was no doubt in his mind that Damian's philandering ways could jeopardize the Reigns family. The best solution was to simply fix the problem and the sooner the better.

Illyassa stroked her long arms and long legs as she cut through the water like a champion swimmer. She attributed twenty laps a day to her perfect physique. Her body was that of a goddess and any man that looked at her once, had to look at her twice and most couldn't take their eyes off of her.

She finished her laps and back stroked to the side of the pool. She grabbed the side railing, dipped her head under the water and began to climb out. No sooner had she looked up and saw three security guards she recognized by name: Yonas, Kaleb, and Negassi.

"What are you idiots doing here? You are trespassing on private property? You do know that?" she began screaming and calling for her own personal team of security that had been assigned by her husband.

"We're here on behalf of the Minister," said Kaleb standing toe to toe with Illyassa holding his hands up as if not to cause harm.

"Whatever, I'm not going anywhere with you," she spat back and I order you to leave these premises now or..."

"Or what?" Negassi interrupted her. He had strict orders from the Minister and a range of options including drugging her if it meant bringing her back safely.

Illyassa knew the men well. They acted on behalf of her father. They never went outside the box when it came to the Minister. *Oh my God, what if Princess has called him already. What if my father knows and he wants to punish me?* Illyassa couldn't help but to think of the Western ways of freedom she had adapted. She knew they were there on behalf of her father, whom she had been avoiding like the plague.

"Come on Illyassa, don't put yourself through it, we're taking you home per order of the Minister," said Negassi as he moved closer to her and grabbed her arm.

"Get your hands off me," she screamed at Negassi before using a Brazilian jujitsu move she learned from her self-defensive training she was forced to learn as a young teenage girl. Her father always wanted her to know how to protect herself. And she could. Illyassa had been trained in various forms of deadly martial arts techniques by her father's military. These men standing in front of her were no match whatsoever. Her father had to know that.

Negassi tried holding her arms behind her back, before she used her foot, bent down and somehow managed to kick him in the groin, the neck and then the chest, as she watched him fall to the ground.

"Is that all you got?" she said to Yonas before snapping his neck and throwing him in the pool to drown. At which time Kaleb came charging towards her, she did a high kick, spun around and ended in back of her assailant where she grabbed his head and was about to twist his neck perfectly when she felt a pinch in the side of her neck. She let Kaleb go just in time. Kaleb turned around and looked at her stopping his attack.

His eyes focused on the shooter who was standing high above them on her own terrace. It was Hakim her friend for many, many, years. Her hand felt the dart as her eyes widened at the sight of Hakim and she ripped the needle from her neck, looking at it in her hand, she immediately felt dizzy, the entire mountain side of the Canyon was zooming by her so fast, it felt like a classic case of vertigo. She dropped the needle to the ground, her head following the sound before she collapsed into Kaleb's arms.

"We got her, let the Minister know, we got her for him and we're bringing her home," ordered the guard holding

Illyassa.

Chapter Twenty One

The meeting was being held at the Bellagio in Las Vegas. Don Tito Bonafacio's limousine pulled up to the private villa of Don Pancrazio. He watched as his butler opened the door. Don Luigi Gianchetta stepped out first, adjusted himself then began to walk inside. Behind him was Don Carlo Cinzia and Don Tito Bonafacio himself. They were there to see Don Vincente Pancrazio who had rented a private and separate villa in a quiet corner of the property. His villa came with a private terrace and pool which was surrounded by topiary shrubs, chaise lounges and outdoor tables. He had his own butler and his own private limousine entrance. His three bedroom villa boasted a kitchen, dining room and fully stocked bar. He had a master bedroom with his and hers bathrooms, steam showers and it came stocked with Hermes products. And let's not mention seven bathrooms and twelve telephones. What more could a Don ask for.

The butler led them inside where Vincente was waiting.

"My friends, my friends, welcome in, welcome in," he ushered waving his arms as he leaned in and kissed both sides of the other Dons faces. "What would you like to drink?" he asked as the butler stood close by ready to take the order.

"Come, I have everything set up on the patio for us.

And he did. A lavish buffet of roasted chicken, filet mignon and salmon grilled in a lemon-garlic butter sauce, along with roasted potatoes, corn soufflé, and asparagus. Then there was the pasta and all the different gravies. And the most delicious crab meat and fresh lobster balls to snack on and an array of breads and pastries.

"I'm so hungry. This looks wonderful," said Don Gianchetta.

"Me too, I haven't eaten since this morning," added Don Bonafacio.

The men got their plates of food, helping themselves as the butler brought glasses of water and glasses of red wine.

After everyone was seated the Dons made a toast to the fallen members of the New York Mafia.

"God bless the dead," said Don Pancrazio raising his glass in the air.

"God bless the dead," said the other Dons in unison.

"Tonight we celebrate the end to all those who've had it coming to them for a long, long time," said Don Pancrazio. "Everything is in place and after tonight the Reigns family will be no more and that Ethiopian son of a bitch who killed Don Gianpaulo Cipriano, Don Nicostrato Cinzia, Don Patrizio Giovanneta, Don Umberto Constantino and let's not forget my brother, Don Marcellino Pancrazio the youngest of my mother's nine sons. God bless them all."

"God bless the dead," they said toasting once more.

"He'll wish he had never set foot on American soil after tonight," said Don Pancrazio before adding. "There's no turning back, the Minister will wish he had never started this war."

"And what about the Reigns family what is to become of them."

"Nothing, they are simply no more," laughed Don Pancrazio as the other's joined in toasting their glasses of wine over and over as they ate their belly's full. "After tonight, they will all be dead."

Chapter Twenty Two

Chief Immanuel Hillel Malaika who was Minister of Intelligence and Minister of the Secret State Security Service for the Federal Democratic Republic of Ethiopia followed closely behind his security detail as they led him down the corridor to the press room where he was scheduled to speak in front of the Council of Ministries in which he was a member. The subject matter was the recent terrorist attacks of Al Qaeda and his new Security Proposal to keep the country safe.

Standing next to him, the secretary to the Minister whispered in his ear.

"The private plane has landed and Illyassa is safe and sound on Ethiopian soil," she said assuringly.

"Thank you, this is wonderful news," he said all smiles before leaving the safety of the red curtain behind. He walked out on the stage and raised his right arm, waving to the council members who cheered his name and clapped for his reign.

"Thank you, thank you, thank you very much," he said as the council members took to their seats. "We are here today with the intent of making our country safe from terrorism. The Secret State Security Service has confirmed that we may be a target for Al Que..." A shot rang out from the inside of the press room and before the security detail could make a move, Minister Malaika fell to the ground, his body shot once in the chest and blood pouring from his back.

"Someone call an ambulance. Minister Malaika has been shot," screamed his secretary who was by his side as the council members began scrambling like cockroaches avoiding bright light. A news reporter filmed live and even had a clip of the actual gun shooting of the Minister. He followed his camera as Minister Malaika's body hit the floor. Of course security locked down the press room, but it was too late, no gun and no suspects were found. Whoever shot the Minister managed to do so from inside the press room without alerting anyone to a weapon and escaping without being noticed.

Emory Reigns walked into the massive eat-in kitchen and sat down.

"Como estas, Senora Reigns?" asked Guadelupe, Emory's personal assistant.

"Oh, I don't know Lupe, I don't know. It's so much going on. What can I say," she said smiling at her live-in companion.

"Oh, Father O'Connell called for you today while you were napping. I meant to tell you when woke up, but the maytag people came and I forgot."

"Oh, I'll call him back tomorrow."

"You like senora?" asked Lupe holding up a chicken empanada.

"Oh yes, I'll take one and some lemonade, please," said Emory wishing she had never moved into Damian's ranch.

"So, when are they moving out of here?" asked Lupe exhausted from the heavy work load.

"I don't know but I sure am ready to go get my own

place. I let Damian talk me into moving here after Davidian died and had I known they'd all be moving back...let's just say I'm thinking about getting a realtor, but don't say a word to anyone," said Emory holding her fingers to her lips animating her story.

"Of course not, senora, do I ever say a word. No, not ever senora, whatever you say to me is just me and you."

Guadelupe passed Emory the empanadas and lemonade.

"I will be back, senora. I go do the laundry now," said Lupe before leaving Emory to herself.

Emory watched as Lupe walked away. *I sure do wish you were here right now,* said Emory talking to her ghost of a husband as she thought of the day he died. It was actually here out in the back yard. They had a family reunion, small but then again nothing with the Reigns family was ever small. Damian had small private chartered planes whisk family members from the larger airports to the ranch's small but modern, airstrip. The ranch proper, sat above a massive underground aquifer, and as such, was one of the few West Texas ranches that remained green all-year around. The fact that three large rivers flowed through the property, did not hurt either.

Damian's sixty-five thousand acre, thirty thousand head of cattle, and acres of brand-new facilities filled to the brim with brand new state-of-the-art equipment, made his operation the envy of ranchers throughout the country. The Reigns Ranch, also known as the Double R Ranch, was a first-class operation, through and through.

The main house was thirty thousand square feet, and contained twenty bedrooms, thirty two bathrooms, six living areas, a massive main dining hall, and an equally massive home theater, and a bowling alley. The seamed metal-roofed structure had been constructed to stand the test of time. It was a post and beam affair, made out of a beautiful white limestone known as Sisterdale Cream, named after the area from which it had been quarried. Inside, massive intertwined antlers had been transformed into beautiful chandeliers, while antiqued, rough-hewn boards salvaged and restored from old Texas barns, covered the floor. The main house was a grand Texas style mansion, decorated in a relaxed elegance.

The ranch was a sportsman and outdoor lover's paradise. Bucks, deer, elk, wild turkeys, hogs, quail, pheasant, and a variety of other game, called the ranch home. They fed near one of the three well-stocked spring-fed lakes or sometimes near one of over a dozen spring-fed creeks located on the property. On the ranch, Damian had constructed regulation-size basketball courts, tennis courts, a clay-shooting field, a football field, and a golf course. It was the football field, however, which held everyone's attention today.

"Go long!" Damian shouted, waving his hands through the air.

Darius Reigns performed a quick shimmy, and then a shake, and then sprinted hurriedly down the field. Damian lobbed the ball through the air, sending it down the field and into the hands of its sprinting recipient.

"Yes!" Darius shouted as he clutched the football and headed into the end zone.

Damian and the rest of his teammates raised their arms and cheered. They ran down the field to the end zone, where they quickly assembled for their celebratory dance.

"Just kick the ball off, will you!" Dante shouted. He turned toward his brother Dajon. "I'll take this one. I'm going to try to run it all the way back on their asses."

"C'mon, kick the ball off, cowards!" Dajon shouted and clapped his hands. He, like Dante, was eager to score and catch up.

Damian and his team lined up just outside the end

zone, and waited impatiently as Zach Reigns kicked the football. The football soared through the air, over the head of Dante and his waiting teammates, and into the hands of a stranger rounding the corner of the house. The stranger was Nathan Hess, and he was surrounded by a large group of G-men.

"Nathan!" Damian shouted furiously. "What in the hell is the meaning of this?"

"Leave this property, immediately!" Dante shouted.

Nathan approached the group of Reigns family members gathering just before him. He stopped just in front of Dante.

"Dante Reigns, it is my distinct pleasure," Nathan Hess smiled, "to announce that you're under arrest, you son of a bitch!"

"Yeah right!" Dante huffed. "Under arrest for what?"

"For the murder of one Dr. Julian Huffington," Nathan informed him. "Now, turn around, and place your hands behind your head."

Emory remembered the day like it was yesterday, her heart pounding as she and Davidian made their way thought the crowd of relatives and approached Nathan.

"Nathaniel Ezekiel Hess, what's the meaning of this?" Emory demanded.

"Em, your son's under arrest," Nathan informed her.

"My boy's under arrest?" Davidian bellowed. "For what?"

Nathan shook his head. "Dee, Em, I've been trying to tell you about your sons for the last eight years. For some reason, you refused to listen. I know that you've heard the gossip, the rumors, and the stories, just like everyone else has. But, for some reason, you refused to listen. Your son's under arrest for murder."

Emory whimpered as tears began to stream down her face.

"Nathan, my boys are innocent!" Davidian shouted. "Damn it, Nathan, why didn't you call me and talk to me first!"

"Dee, I and the entire world, have been trying to talk to you about your children," Nathan responded. "How could the two of you have been so blind?"

"Blind?" Davidian shouted. "Blind to what, blind to their success, blind to their education, blind to what?"

"Your children have created a drug empire that stretches across half the country!" Nathan shouted. "They have murdered, maimed, bribed, coerced, and cajoled their way to the top of a drug Commission so notorious, so bloody, and so ruthless, that it defies description!"

"Bullshit!" Davidian shouted. "I know what this is about, Nathan! This is about a father getting revenge for his daughter! This is about nothing more than Damian and Stacia!"

Nathan threw his head back in laughter. "Dee, you cannot possibly be that stupid."

"Let it go, Nathan!" Davidian shouted. "Stacia has moved on; why haven't you?"

"Dee, this is about a daughter all right," Nathan shouted. "But not about mine. It's about your daughter, Princess, and about the number of bodies that she has left scattered all throughout the country. It's about a son, Dante. A son so murderous, so ruthless, so damn cold and calculating, that he makes Satan blush! And a son, Damian, who had the entire world at his feet. A son who could have done so much good, a son who could have been great, who could have been a senator, a governor or anything that he wanted to be. A son who used his brilliance to bring death and destruction to his own people. Your children, Dee, whose activities and personalities and lives you're ultimately responsible for. The blood on their hands is also on yours.

You raised these coldhearted murderous bastards."

"Nathaniel Ezekiel Hess!" Emory shouted. "That's quite enough!"

"Nathan!" Davidian shouted. "Nathan." Davidian clutched his chest. "Nathan."

"Dad!" Damian shouted.

Davidian clutched at his chest and fell to the ground.

"Davidian!" Emory dropped to her knees and cradled her husband.

"Paramedics, get the paramedics here quick!" Nathan shouted.

A group of uniformed FBI men dressed in black combat gear removed their helmets, dropped to their knees, and begin to work on Davidian. One pressed on Dravidian's chest, while the other breathed into his mouth.

Nathan lifted his handheld communicator. "Eagle One, this is Command; get that bird on the ground right now. We need an emergency transport to the hospital."

Princess pushed her way through the crowd, knelt down by her father, and stared up at Nathan. "This is your fault."

"I was just doing my job," Nathan told her.

"If he dies," Princess told him. "The gloves come off."

The number of limousines that lined the cemetery was reminiscent of Mann's Chinese Theater during Oscar night. There were hundreds of them; Maybach limousines, Mercedes limousines, BMW limousines, Lincoln Town Car limousines, Rolls Royce limousines, and dozens upon dozens of long, black Cadillac limousines. A phalanx of black-suited patrons lined up just in front of the Reigns family, to pay their respects to Davidian, and to pass along their condolences to Emory and to the rest of the Reigns family. It was a procession that stretched for several hundred yards throughout the massive Catholic cemetery.

The casket of Davidian Reigns had been constructed of titanium, surrounded by intricately carved imported African ebony. Tufts of imported hand-woven Persian silk lined the interior, and highly polished chrome accents and inlays tastefully decorated the exterior of the coffin. It was clear to everyone in attendance, that the family had spent tens of thousands of dollars, just on the box alone.

Roses draped the coffin, and covered the table upon which it sat, giving the illusion that the coffin sat upon a massive bed of flowers. The cemetery itself was Catholic through and through, but it was also very private. The Reigns family had been devout Catholics for as far back as anyone could remember, and this was the family's very own private cemetery. It sat on several acres, within the confines of the Reigns family's large South Central Texas hill country ranch, and held a commanding hilltop view of several beautiful hills, valleys, and creeks. It was without a doubt, a beautiful place to spend one's eternal resting days.

Emory sat between her four sons, with Dante sitting on the end next to two U.S. Marshals. Princess sat on the other side of her mother, holding her hand and comforting her. Even beneath her massive black Chanel hat and black Chanel sunglasses, one could sense her seething, fiery anger.

Davidian had been more than the patriarch of a large, clan; he had been the wisdom, the light, and the love of an entire generation of nieces and nephews. He was the father with the kind words of encouragement. He was the uncle who made everyone laugh. He was the father who preached the importance of education. He was the one with the sunshine smile, who always had shiny quarters when the ice-cream truck rounded the corner. He was a marvelous father to his children and loyal loving husband to his wife.

Emory missed Davidian. So much that she often cried her self to sleep. Princess burst through the French doors that led to the kitchen.

"Oh, hello mother, how are you?" asked Princess kissing her mother on the cheek.

"I'm fine, where's your brothers?"

"Well, last check Damian wanted everyone to meet him at Phillipes for a celebration. Didn't you hear?"

"Hear what?"

"He's found the cure for AIDS."

"Are you kidding me?"

"No mother, this is big, really, really big!" exclaimed Princess knowing that she had to use a little extra energy to get Emory riled up. "Come on, put on something cute and let's bunny hop our tails down to Phillipe Chows," said Princess leaving her mother with no choice. Emory smiled at Princess and Princess smiled back. "Come on, mother, let's go."

Just then automatic weapons could be heard and shots were being fired just outside the ranch windows. A bullet shattered the glass to the kitchen window.

"Mother, get down, now," said Princess as she dropped to the floor.

"Lupe could be heard screaming to the top of her lungs in Spanish, a simple gun shot silenced her. There were at least fifty guards assigned to the ranch by Brandon Reigns. However, there were one hundred and fifty men storming the premises there to kill anyone they could.

"Mother, come," said Princess as she waved to her mother to follow her. Maybe it was the gun shots, maybe it was the fear of not knowing, maybe it was older age that had slowed her reflexes. Whatever it was it cost Emory dearly, as she lifted herself up a gun man entered the kitchen, pointing an automatic at Emory's moving body.

"Noooo," screamed out Princess shooting her .32 in his direction. She hit him, but not before his bullet pierced into Emory's stomach. "Mommy, noooo," said Princess as she fired at the gun man until his body dropped to the ground.

She ran over to her mother who was unbelievably still standing.

"Mother, are you okay?" asked Princess looking into her eyes before seeing the blood rushing from Emory's wound. "Oh my God," said Princess before Emory fell to the floor. "Oh mother, please, oh God," said Princess as she pulled out her cell phone dialing Dante.

"Hello," he said answering his cell.

"Dante," screamed Princess as a bullet pierced her shoulder and knocked her over, the phone falling out her hand. They moved quickly and continued killing and wounding the security detail outside as they murdered the hired housekeeping staff inside the house looking for the rest of the family members.

Off in the distance sirens could be heard and through the ear pieces everyone was ordered out of the house. Within minutes they were gone. Gigantic helicopters from miles away zoomed in and picked up the gunmen just as fast as they had zoomed in, landed, and dropped them off. It was a successful hit, a very successful hit.

On a sunny beach in Key Largo off the Florida Keys Don Pancrazio swung in a hammock on his secluded tropical private paradise featuring his own private lagoon and ocean front dock with boat lift. It was the perfect place to call home, only a hop, skip and a jump from the Miami International Airport.

Don Pancrazio sipped on an Arnold Palmer and cozied to the warm breeze.

His telephone rang and he quickly answered anticipating the call. He smiled then placed the phone back into the cradle.

"For you, brother, may they all burn in hell," he said

laughing as he sipped at his drink.

Chapter Twenty Three

Dante dropped the phone as he looked down at Angela. His instincts had his mind racing a thousand miles a minute. *Not the ranch, not Princess, what of our mother, where is Damian?* So many questions flooded his acuity he couldn't think clearly. His phone rang again as he dashed from the hospital room down the corridor and to the elevator doors. His two team security detail following footsteps behind him.

"Hold that!" he ordered as he squeezed his body sideways through the closing doors causing them to re-open. He hit the close button, and tried to remain calm and smooth as he watched the doors close. He pressed the L button for the lobby but the elevator stopped on three picked up a guy carrying an oxygen tank and then finally delivered Dante and his guards to the lobby.

"Sir, is everything okay," asked his driver, Benny who was smoking a cigarette outside the car.

"No, there's been a hit on the family ranch," Dante said running right by Benny who quickly picked up his pace and followed him.

Dante ran all the way to his car which was parked off to the side of the entrance.

"Let me drive!" he ordered as he hopped into the driver's seat of a Maybach leaving his driver Benny standing on the side of the road left behind.

"What the fu..." he couldn't get it out fast enough. Dante had slammed the door in his face and was speeding away from him before he could get in the back seat.

He drove straight to the Reign's Family Ranch. Police cars, ambulance vehicles and even a fire truck had all been dispensed. He pulled up and parked next to a silver Lincoln Towncar. He hopped out the car and right into the hands of Nathan Hess, the Federal Bureau of Investigations Special Agent in Charge.

"Whoa, slow down, son," said Nathan after walking through the blood strewn crime scene.

"Son? Did you just call me son?" questioned Dante as he looked dead smack into the eyes of the man who he blamed for killing his father.

"Dante, please, I can't let you in there."

"That's my house Nathan, not yours."

"No, that's my crime scene. I got dead bodies from one end of the house to the other. Trust me, you don't want to go in there."

"Where's Princess? Where's my mother?" he said as guilt quickly replaced his dislike for Nathan Hess.

"Dante, I'm so sorry. I'm very sorry," said Nathan already knowing the war the Reigns family was battling. Nathan Hess was FBI he knew everything he wanted to know when he wanted and needed to know it.

Dante used his force and pushed Nathan Hess into the ground and ran into the side door of the family ranch. The ranch had been destroyed by the gunman. Every square inch demolished with gun fire from the automatic weapons they used. A gurney brushed by him carrying Carlos one of the gardeners. Just as he saw his mother's body being loaded onto a gurney by two other paramedics.

"Mom! Mom! No, mom can you hear me?" he said running over to her side.

"I'm sorry, sir," said a young brunette wearing white

pants and a white over coat. "She didn't make it," said the girl as she stepped back and away from Dante allowing him to see that his mother was in fact dead.

"No, mom, no, not mom," he said as he cradled Emory's lifeless body in his arms, holding her head in his arms.

"Dante, I am sorry but we have to let these people do their job," said Nathan as he put his hand on Dante's shoulder.

"Their job? What fucking job, Nathan? What fucking job? It's because of you, you fucking FBI, you probably knew they were coming, that's why you're here now."

"Dante, I heard it on my scanner. I'm not here on official business. I'm here because I know your family. I thought I might be able to help. But, the FBI has no jurisdiction over this crime scene. This is for the state boys to handle."

Dante looked at Nathan Hess, for all he knew Nathan would be pulling out an arrest warrant at any moment taking him down to FBI headquarters. But, then again as he looked around, there were no other FBI agents in the room only locals.

"Where's Princess?"

"She was shot up pretty bad, Dante. They've already taken her by ambulance to the hospital."

"Where's Damian?"

"I haven't seen him. Come on, let me get you to the hospital."

"I can drive myself, Nathan."

"Yeah, but I've got lights and sirens. You ride with me," said Nathan knowing that Dante was mourning his mother and in no state to drive.

Nathan got him to the hospital and handed him a card. Here's my cell phone Dante. If you need anything just call me."

Dante took the card from Nathan. He appreciated the gesture but still couldn't trust the man. Stacia's father or not, the man was still FBI.

Dante sped through the Emergency Room double doors as they magically opened and closed behind him.

"May I help you, sir?" asked a young blonde woman sitting behind the nurse's station.

"I'm looking for my sister, Princess Reigns," said Dante as he spotted Pedros from Damian's security detail. "Pedros, Pedros," he called out as he rushed toward him.

"Oh senor Reigns, I am so sorry, senor."

"Where's Damian, where's my brother?"

"Senor, no one tell you, there was an explosion, a bomb in his car and he's..." said Pedros shaking his head as he wiped tears from his eyes.

"He's what? He's dead?" asked Dante fearing the worse.

"No, he's not dead, he's in the room right there, sir. But, wait, I must warn you, sir, he's..."

Before Pedros could finish his sentence Dante was already by Damian's bed side.

"Oh god," he said as he saw his brother. Damian's head was wrapped as if wearing a turban, his face and parts of his body badly burned and wrapped. His leg was in a cast and lifted above his torso held in place by a sling.

"Damian, can you hear me? Damian, I'm here. Can you hear me?" said Dante squeezing his brother's hand.

"He's in a coma. He may be able to hear you. We have yet to determine whether the subconscious mind allows a patient to comprehend voices while in a comatose state. I'm Dr. Watkins," the doctor said extending his hand to Dante. "Are you an immediate relative?" the doctor asked ready to excuse anyone who wasn't.

"I'm his brother," said Dante saddened.

"You're brother has suffered a very massive head

injury. We are running tests to see if there is any bruising or swelling of the brain tissue. We've performed a cat scan and he had no fractures to his skull. He's breathing on his own, which is very good. And we've ruled out damage to his brainstem and spinal cord, so that rules out paralysis. So, once the tests come back, I'm hoping that we'll know exactly what we're dealing with but there was no blood on his brain when we ran the cat-scan which is excellent.

"What about the burns and his leg."

"The burns will heal, only third degree. It just looks really, really bad, and he has a broken leg. We casted him and he'll be fine, maybe on crutches when he wakes up, but the burns and the leg aren't why he's being transported to ICU, it's his unconscious state that concerns me. We don't want him like that for too long. He needs to wake up and the sooner the better."

Dante turned back to his brother and stared down at his lifeless face.

"I need you Damian, come on, brother, wake up."

Just as the doctor was reaching the doorway, he noticed the four armed guards stationed outside Damian Reigns room.

"Excuse me, can you tell me how to find my sister, Princess Reigns?"

"Is she a patient here at the hospital?"

"Yes, that's what I was informed."

"Give me her name, I'll ask the nurse's station to find her for you."

"Princess Reigns," said Dante as he nodded to the doctor to go find his sister. He turned back to his brother and thought of his mother. Her body was so lifeless and her face in shock. He remembered cradling her blood stained clothing and looked down at his shirt which was covered in her blood as well.

"Excuse me, Mr. Reigns, Dr. Watkins wanted me to

tell you that your sister is in the Wallace Wing on the third floor in room 217," said a young, slim blonde no more than twenty five.

"Thank you," said Dante. He turned to the guards standing vigil outside Damian's room.

"Don't let anyone in except Dr. Watkins and this nurse right here. I don't care who they say they are. No one gets in to my brother."

"Gotcha boss," said Sylvester the head of the four man team assigned to protect Damian.

Dante walked quickly with one of the security detail following closely behind him. He stepped off the elevator of the Wallace Wing and walked down the hall to room 217, where Pedros had positioned another four man security team outside her door.

"Princess," Dante spoke softly standing above her. She had undergone surgery and had the bullet removed from her shoulder. Her arm was in a sling, her body positioned upright, peacefully sedated, quietly resting. "Princess," he said again as she opened her eyes.

She looked up at him, tears in her eyes. "Mother was mur..." she couldn't finish without breaking in to tears. "There was nothing I could do, they came so fast, Dante," she said crying to him as he held her head in his hands.

"I know, Princess, I know," he said his strong hands cradling her head. "Damian was hit. He's here in the hospital. He's in a coma," said Dante.

Princess looked up at Dante, his hands still holding her face. "Not Damian, Dante. Not Damian."

Chapter Twenty Four

The Minister looked out of the window on the 47th Floor of the St. Regis Hotel. He had been taken there shortly after the assassination attempt.

"Who is this idiot you people found to be my replacement. If he says one more word to the media I will kill him myself," shouted the Minister as he watched CNN. The coverage of his failed assassination had been covered around the globe. And right now every news reporter in the free world wanted an up close and personal interview with the Minister.

"He was chosen by the Council, your greatness," said a humbling member of the Minister's cabinet.

Minister Malaika paced back and forth in the hotel suite. Too much had happened in the last forty eight hours. He watched carefully at the footage CNN presented showing the botched assassination attempt. If not for the poor soul lying in the hospital pretending to be him, he could be a dead man. He already knew who to blame. *Those fools have no idea what they have done. They might try to attack the Reigns family, but I'm not them and neither is my army.*

A knock at the door silenced his thoughts of revenge.

"Enter," the Minister ordered.

As the door opened, a tired and angry Illyassa was carried into the suite by two men on each side of her.

"We had to drug her, she killed Yonas, sir. We cleaned everything up, sir."

The Minister put up his hand waving for silence. He did not want to hear the sordid details of what happened. The only thing that mattered to him was that his daughter was safe from harm and was where she needed to be and had been safely returned home.

"Father, I can't believe you would do this to me."

"Illyassa, this is for your own good. If they would try to assassinate me, do you think you might be in danger?"

Illyassa looked at her father and decided now would be as good as any a time to tell him she was filing for divorce from Damian.

"I do not love him. I can not be his wife. I am filing for divorce."

Minister Malaika already knew that his daughter didn't love Damian. But, he thought that married life would suit her and she'd grow into the position of loving wife as most women did.

"And what of Damian?" the Minister frowned.

"He said okay and that he just wants me to be happy," she lied not knowing what Damian felt.

"If you are not in love with him, then you should not have to share his bed, Illyassa."

"Thank you," she said as she kissed her father and sat next to him.

Just then the doors to the St. Regis Hotel suite opened. "Sir, it is time we go. You must switch places with the replacement."

"Now at this very moment?" the Minister questioned, as if they couldn't see him talking to his daughter.

"Yes sir, the sooner the better, we need to get you to the hospital as quickly as possible. The replacement has passed away, sir."

"Oh, well yes, I can see then why we should be on our way. We don't need the countryside believing I'm dead," the Minister laughed as he patted Hakeem, his loyal and trusting confidant.

"Exactly, sir," smiled Hakeem as he led the Minister out of the suite.

Princess slept through the nightmares of her mother being gunned down in front of her. She saw the shooter's face and she saw her mother's body fall to the floor. Night after night, the same dreams, the same haunting images. With the death of her mother, her family would never be the same. *If only I could control time.* Timing was everything in her world. She lifted herself from the side of the bed and refreshed. Every morning that she had been in the hospital, she would wake and go to Damian. She had sat vigil by Damian's bedside ever since the car bombing.

"Father O'Connell wants to know when we want to have the services for mother," Dante said as he strolled through Damian's hospital door.

"Shouldn't we wait until Damian comes around?"

"Princess, must I answer that?" said Dante realistically. Father O'Connell wants to schedule her services for this Friday afternoon. I've called Dajon and Darius and everyone knows."

"I just can't believe it. I can't believe that mo..."

"Me neither," snapped Dante not wanting the burden of his mother's death discussed. You know that was my Fiorno they blew up?"

"What are you talking about, Dante?"

"My car, my Ferrari, my Fiorno, I let Damian have it and out of all the cars he has, that's the one they put explosives in."

"Your Ferrari? The black one?"

"Yeah, the black one," said Dante as he watched the discovery channel appear on his sister's face.

"Oh, God...oh God," said Princess her hands now cradling her face as she paced a circle in the hospital room.

"What?" Dante asked already knowing something was very wrong with the picture.

"Oh, God, I thought that was your car. I...I..."

"You what?"

"I thought you got rid of it."

"No, I gave it to Damian after you tried to blo..."

Dante, stopped mid sentence thinking of yester year when his demon sister's mission in life was to take him out.

"You blew up Dam...?"

"Oh, God, I feel horrible. I would have never...I thought you got rid of that car. Why didn't you get rid of it?"

"He wanted it," said Dante looking at his brother. "I've heard enough. I'm going to see Angela."

"Oh, God, Dante, what have I done?"

"You want me to answer that?"

"Damian, I'm so sorry, I'm so sorry," said Princess as she fell over onto his chest.

"Do you feel safe?" Dante asked looking at Damian. "I will get you more security brother. Pedros, vien."

'Shut up, you idiot," spat Princess as she slapped Dante's chest.

"Seriously, you fuck his wife, you blow up his car, you leave him comatosed, I mean really, Princess, is there anything else you can knowingly or unknowingly do to this man we call brother."

"Dante, whatever, you know it was an accident. And I only fucked his wife because you made me do it."

"And I made you blow him up too?"

"Pretty much, think about it. Technically, it's your

fault too. You gave him the car."

"You're sick and you know it. Good thing we're here at the hospital."

"Yeah, good thing," said Princess before turning back to Damian. "Poor thing, I'm so sorry, Damian," she said stroking his forehead. "I promise I will make it up to you. I promise."

"Excuse me," said Dr. Holland as he made his way into Damian's room.

"Dr. Holland is everything alright with Angela?" asked Dante.

"Oh, yes, she's stable. I wanted to speak with you about your brother. Daniella visited my office yesterday. She says that Damian is a prime candidate for electro-wave stimulation. Daniella feels that we should try the machine sooner versus later and I want to talk to you about the possibilities of us performing the wave stimuli on Damian. After all, he is the founding father of this miraculous technology."

"What if it doesn't work? Can it hurt him?" asked Princess.

"Well, we're not sure of the possibilities because we've never tried it before on humans," said Dr. Holland, not sure how to answer the question. Our first subject was going to be Angela after the birth of course. But, honestly there's no telling what could happen."

"Oh jeez, that's great. Haven't you tested it on animals or something?" questioned Princess.

"Well, the results weren't positive when we performed the experiments on several chimpanzees but that doesn't mean it won't be successful for Damian."

"What happened to the chimpanzees?" Princess asked.

"They died, the brain waves were too strong, and caused their brain tissue to swell, but I can assure you, on a human, that won't be possible. No, I'm very confidant, this will work, very confident indeed."

Princess and Dante looked at each other, then at Dr. Holland shaking his head with absolute certainty, then at Damian lying silently still.

"Let me think about it, Dr. Holland," said Dante.

"Yes, let us sleep on it," said Princess, rolling her eyes at Dante before looking at Dr. Holland as if he were the biggest quack she'd ever met.

"Okay, folks, I'll talk to you tomorrow," he said before turning and walking out the room. "But remember we're losing the battle the longer he stays asleep."

Princess watched as the strange and weird looking Dr. Holland walked out the door and down the hall. There was something about him Princess didn't like. His bedside manner was too far removed. Dr. Holland was a scientist, before he was a doctor, and genius at that.

"You trust that quack? Where in the hell did he come from?"

"Damian," Dante said as if 'who else', flipping through a Robb Report, stopping at an ad for Christensen Yachts. "God, I wish I was on the Primadonna right now with my wife, sailing the Mediterranean."

"Um...excuse me, reality," said Princess waving her hand, snapping her finger. "You are actually planning on using that experimental heeby jeeby machine on Angela?"

"What choice do I have? Damian said that it was the only possible way to bring her back."

"And you want to use it on Damian?"

"It's his machine. Besides, that quack my dear, sweet, sister is a Bio One scientific expert. All this heeby jeeby experimental machinery is owned and controlled by Damian. If he believes in it, why shouldn't we? Besides, what choice do we have?"

Chapter Twenty Five

Just as she was turning to leave, Stacia Hess appeared in the doorway of Damian's hospital room.

"Oh my God, Damian," she said as she rushed by his bed side.

"Hello, Stacia," said Princess watching as her brother's life long lover fell into pieces at the sight of him. *Oh God, I can't take it*, Princess thought as Stacia began to cry. It was Stacia's father who just so happened to be Nathan Hess, Special FBI Agent in Charge of terrorizing their Reigns Family Empire, putting Dante in jail, causing Damian to marry that ridiculous Illyassa woman, and causing their father, God rest his soul, to drop dead of a heart attack. *There can't be peace, ever with her or her father*, Princess thought to herself. *What is she doing here?*

"Hello, Princess. Hello, Dante," said Stacia to Damian's brother and Damian's sister. She could tell she was the last person wanted in that room.

"I'm so sorry about Ms. Emory, really, I am. And Angela, I'm so sorry for you Dante," said Stacia.

"Thank you," said Dante short and sweet. He thought of Nathan Hess, the FBI, and that one man's determination to undermine the criminal organization of the Reigns family and topple the Reigns Empire. If it weren't for Damian falling

135

in love with Nathan Hess' daughter, Stacia would have been kidnapped and fed to the lion's piece by piece for all the years of turmoil Nathan Hess had caused them. But, Damian loved her and Dante couldn't touch her. *She'd make the perfect revenge for you Nathan Hess, the perfect revenge.*

Dante looked at Princess and she looked back. They could read each other's minds. It was canny to say the least the way they communicated without even saying a word.

No, Dante thought to his sister as he slowly shook his head no at her.

"Have the funeral arrangements been made for Ms. Em?" Stacia asked in all sincerity.

"Dajon and his wife are handling the services. I believe it will be on Friday. Of course, you'll be contacted," said Princess.

"Thank you," she smiled sweetly feeling so sorry for the two of them, especially Dante, his wife, his mother, his brother, all at one time, was just too much for anyone.

Just then Grace appeared.

"Wow, I see the gangs all here!" she stated standing in the doorway.

Princess couldn't stand the local police, let alone FBI agents. *How could he sleep with her? How?* Princess just didn't understand Damian in that regard. But, Damian had a zest for creating complicated situations. The simple, mundane and ordinary just didn't cut it; no matter how beautiful, petite or charming. If you weren't a possible enemy or someone he needed to control, watch, or use then your chances were slim with Damian Reigns. And that was the crazy part about his relationship madness. Love had nothing to do with his chemistry, love was secondary.

Princess took one look at Grace, *this bat, look at her. Look at her hair. She looks like the fucking FBI. Get a makeover why don't you? Jesus, Damian is insane, why doesn't he just fuck the entire police academy next time?*

"I'm going back to my room Dante. My shoulder is bothering me."

"Well, Princess, you know it's always ni...then again...never mind, rest well," said Grace smiling from ear to ear. "Hope your shoulder gets better."

Is this bitch serious? Princess just looked at her, then at Dante.

"Rest, Princess, time to rest," said Dante as he placed his hand on his sister's other shoulder.

"Grace should be dismembered, her body never found and that other one, too," Princess whispered as the two of them turned around to see Grace standing on one side of the bed, Stacia on the other and both of them whimpering, petting, and sniffling over Damian's lifeless body. "You can't be serious?" she muttered before turning for goodnight.

Chapter Twenty-Six

Father O'Connell presided over the services for Emory Reigns. It was a lovely, well planned service. Every detail had been thought of, no expense had been spared. Dajon, Darius, Dante and Princess sat in the second row of pews. Damian would miss his mother's funeral, he would be her only child who wouldn't get a chance to say goodbye.

Jeremiah's brother, Deacon sat next to Dante, his children, Mina and Brandon sat on the other side of him. Grace was present, next to her, Lil D as the family was beginning to call him and Stacia was there with Damian's children Victor, Victoria, Damiana and Damon. To say the least, the resemblance was remarkable. The boys favored their mother's side, but the girls looked like Damian had spit them out himself, both beautiful, both young, and both growing up rich and famous. Their last name was Rodgers after Michael, but the plan was to tell them the truth and give them the Reigns family name. Stacia's divorce from Michael would be finalized within the next few weeks. Her plan was for her and Damian to tell them together. She prayed every day that he'd miraculously wake up. Sitting next to Stacia was her father, Nathan Hess, who Princess wished she could reach around and choke to death.

Dajon had his wife, Antoinette, his children DJ and Cheyenne. Even Illyassa had showed up for her mother-in-law's funeral service. Her main mission was to square away things with Princess and personally deliver the divorce papers that merely required Damian's signature. Under the circumstances, Dante would sign as his legal Power of Attorney. *He'll be happy I did this for him. Now, he can go back to safely sleeping with every America's Next Top Model he wants to.*

For Dante, he didn't need that image of perfect. He just simply needed. Angela was his soul mate. She was all he needed. She was all he wanted. Past physical beauty, she was perfect in every way, to say the least. Deep down inside he knew she would come back to him. He didn't know how he knew it, but he did.

As Father O'Connell began the Lord's Prayer, he asked that everyone in attendance repeat after him. The cream colored casket made of titanium was being lowered into the ground. Dante stood perfectly still, mourning the loss of his mother, Emory Reigns. She had been a wonderful mother, caring wife, and an outstanding role model for her children. It was then, as the casket was being lowered that Dante squeezed Princess' hand. He looked at his sister, the tears streaming down her face. Not even when they were young could he say he remembered her crying, not even once. She was always busy making everyone else around her cry. But, not today, Dante could honestly say that the death of their mother broke his sister's heart. He imagined Damian and how he would handle losing their mother. He imagined Damian not speaking, for many, many days. It was how he himself felt. It took every bit of strength he could muster to simply hold a conversation and the lump that was in his throat just wouldn't go away, no matter how many times he swallowed. The loss was immense, the pain immeasurable.

As the Mercedes Benz stretch limousine pulled up, Dante opened the door for his sister.

"I'm riding with Dajon," Darius could be heard speaking, but Dante didn't respond. Dante would never, ever be able to respond to Darius, but he would protect his secret because Darius was his mother's child and he was his brother's keeper. Deep down Dante loved him, he just wouldn't tolerate him. Therefore, he wouldn't speak to him. Darius was comfortable with his relationship with Dante. He would speak to Dante out of respect, but he was personally satisfied with the fact that Dante refused to accept his lifestyle. Darius cared to the extent that he didn't want to disappoint anyone, but the truth was he didn't appreciate Dante having him put under investigation, his phones, his home, his work environment sabotaged and spied on. But, Dante had done that to Darius for years. However, the information that he gathered, he never revealed. That was just Dante, a part of the character of his self. He only said what needed to be said, nothing more. Not even Princess or Damian knew of Darius' homosexuality, but once Dante figured out who his brother really was, he gave him ground rules and an ultimatum. Darius accepted and followed through and Dante respected that much about him, nothing else though, just that he followed Dante's command. What Darius didn't know though was that to this very day, Darius, his partners, and everything about his life was watched, listened to, and followed. Darius thought once Dante had confronted him, he had stopped his medaling, eavesdropping, and wiring, but Dante never did and he never would, not with Darius's lifestyle. God forbid Darius ever take his clothes off, exposing multiple piercings and body artwork. God forbid Princess find out, let alone Mr. Playboy, Damian. No, Dante would continue to keep Darius under wing and monitor his life style, his friends, lovers, and all the other weirdo things that Darius subjected himself to, just as a precaution and Darius would continue to live like a man by day and something, somewhere between a transy and a sexual deviant homosexual by night.

Dante sat inside the limousine as the driver closed the

door. He watched as one security guard sat in the front seat with the driver and the other security guards piled into big, black, suburbans with dark black tinted windows. Travel, after Angela, had changed drastically. Princess stared out the window silently. Dante's phone began to ring and she looked over at him.

He looked back at her recognizing the number. He held up his finger telling her to pay attention.

"Yes, Oso, this is Dante Reigns."

She listened carefully to him, as he paid close attention to the caller and what he was saying.

"Thank you very much for your condolences."

"I want to meet with you, Dante. We have much to discuss," said Oso on the other line.

Dante knew exactly what Oso was calling for. He wanted the war to stop. And with the recent deaths of their mother and his wife, it was no wonder that calls from all over the world were pouring in. No one wanted a war. The other heads of state were concerned and the Dons outside of New York were concerned. So to say the least the trickle down effect of war affected everybody. And the last person it would affect would be Oso. He had come into his power with the death of El Jeffe and he had no intention of small turf wars with heads of state and Dons continue. He was determined that the death, the violence, and the back and forth between the two for greed and power must stop.

Dante hung up the phone, the arrangements were made. He would make the trip to Columbia, alone.

"I want to go with you," said Princess as she layed her hand on top of her brothers.

"No, I want you to stay back here. You are my eyes and ears and you must watch over Damian. I will be fine," he said hoping his psychology worked.

Princess turned her head and looked out the window of the moving limousine. She wanted to take the meeting.

"I don't understand. You don't even want the business, Dante. Damian doesn't want it either. He wants Bio One. I've been fighting everyone for years. I just don't understand, you know that I've always wanted to be the boss, please let me go with you," she said the whole time staring out the window, never once looking at him.

"I need you here," said Dante softly, sitting to her right looking out of the limousine window, never once looking at her.

Chapter Twenty Seven

Daniella and Dr. Holland decided that it would be best if Damian were transported back to Bio One. A room had been fitted for Damian and Dr. Holland would be able to offer him all the benefits of being in a hospital and then some.

"I just don't think we should do the procedure here. Unlike, Angela, he can be moved," Dr. Holland explained to Princess. "Trust me," he added before he ordered a team of six men to carefully lift Damian onto a gurney and then into a Bio One ambulance.

Trust you? This is bad, Princess thought as she watched the orderlies lift her brother's lifeless body onto a gurney before strolling him out of the room.

"When do you think you are going to perform the procedure?" asked Princess.

"First thing in the morning," said Dr. Holland full of certainty.

"First thing in the morning?" Princess questioned as if she hadn't heard him the first time. She watched as Daniella and Dr. Holland walked around Damian's hospital room. Daniella took notes from his hospital charts while Dr.

143

Holland checked all the monitors and hospital equipment.
"I think we're ready," said Dr. Holland.

"Yes, doctor, we are," said Daniella matter of factly.
"Are you coming with us?" asked Daniella catching Princess
off guard.

"Umm...I have a stop to make, but I'll be right behind
you," answered Princess.

Just as Daniella was leaving the room Stacia Hess
appeared.

"Where's Damian? What happened to him?"
questioned Stacia as she looked at Daniella then Princess.

"He's being moved to Bio One," responded Princess.

"Why, what for?"

"We have medical treatments that are more advanced
and far outweigh that of modern medicine. He will receive the
most advanced treatments in the world at Bio One. His
chances of coming out of the coma are one hundred
percent," answered Daniella.

"Well, can I see him?" asked Stacia not wanting to
waste any time.

"He's being transported now, once we get him
stabilized, he can have visitors," she said smiling at Stacia
realizing that the woman in front of her wasn't just a friend.
Daniella could tell that Stacia was a little more special than
a friend. How special, Daniella didn't know. But Stacia's
concern seemed more out of love, than anything else.

"Okay, fine, I'll see you guys over at Bio One. I might
not be able to get back today, but I'll stop by tomorrow,"
Stacia told Princess.

"We'll be there," smiled Princess as Stacia said her
goodbyes.

"Who was that?"

"She is a long time friend of Damian's. They grew up
together," said Princess as if Stacia was nothing more than a

neighbor.

"Oh," said Daniella knowing they had to be more than friends by the way Stacia acted.

"She also has four children...with Damian," smiled Princess as if children were like plants they had grown together.

"Ohhh," said Daniella wondering if Damian was in love with her.

"Yeah, that's who she is," smiled Princess. "I'll see you later at Bio One," Princess said leaving Daniella standing in the middle of Damian's hospital room looking confused and unsure.

Dante showered, dressed in a William Fioravanti suit and packed a black Louis Vutton Comanche. He had thought of every detail and possible aspect of the trip Oso had asked him to make. *I shouldn't be going alone,* he told himself. But then again, Oso had ordered that he come alone. So, what choice was he left with? His security detail was stationed inside and outside the 14,000 square foot home he had shared with Angela. He looked around the Italian marble bathroom, it was just as it was the night they had went to Damian's gala at Bio One, the night of the accident. A pair of panty hose layed on the bathroom floor, their towels, clothes still on the floor of his closet, her closet; forget about it, their bed, an oversized king, all seemed like yesterday. It wasn't yesterday, though. Months had passed and no one had been there, not even the cleaning people. After the accident, he moved into Damian's ranch that had been the family compound. But now, after the invasion, everything had a bullet hole in it. To the extent, the house would be demolished and rebuilt, if rebuilt. But no doubt, it would be demolished. He thought of his mother, his father, his brother, his wife. Much had been gained in their quest for vast wealth, but then again, so much had been lost. Even with the money, the riches, and the lavish luxurious lifestyle, a part of Dante held much regret. *What could I give to bring them back? One day, Angela, one day, I live here only to see you again?* He held a size seven Manolo Blahnik in his hand, a three inch heeled, pink lace slipper. He sat the shoe on the island inside her closet and grabbed his Commanche bag. He turned the light off to their bedroom and walked down the hall where his security detail was waiting for him.

"Ready, sir," a big, husky, black guy from Nebraska everyone called Big Boom asked him.

"No, Big Boom, not really," Dante said as Big Boom took his luggage and followed closely behind him.

They made it to San Antonio International Airport in record speed. Security had called ahead, everything was arranged. Air Reigns One was being surveyed by the ground crew and would be fully stocked for their trip to and from. Dante always made sure the plane was overlooked before take off. He didn't need to get in the air to realize anything was wrong. He had the same pilot, the same co-pilot and the same flight crew as usual. His security detail would fly with him, and wait for his return at the airport. They had phones, walkie talkies, and pagers to stay in constant contact.

He called Princess as he boarded Air Reigns One.

"It's me, I'm on One," said Dante. "We should be there in eight hours. I'll call you when we land."

"Sounds good, everything is fine. I checked on Angela and I'm heading to Bio One now to see Damian. I have Pedros outfitting a security detail for me and I'm going home tonight. I miss home."

"Yeah, I miss mine, too," said Dante thinking of the pink, lacey, Manolo slipper.

He hung up the phone and seated himself at a table. The wood grain finish of the chairs and consuls had been cleaned and the plane's tan leather smelled brand new. A flight plan for International travel usually took days to clear. However, Dante had his flight plan cleared within a couple of hours.

"Hello, Mr. Reigns, may I get you anything?"

He looked up at Lori and Paige, his stewardesses.

"Hi, Mr. Reigns, how are you feeling? I got you a pillow," said Paige as she placed the tiny neck pillow gently behind his head.

"Hi, girls how are you?" asked Dante looking at the two blondes smiling, giggly, and waiting to serve him, literally.

"We're good," they said sounding like the Bopsy Twins.

"I'm so sorry about Mrs. Reigns," said Lori.

"I know, oh my God, Mr. Reigns are you okay?" Paige said leaning her perfect size C breasts into him and giving him a hug.

"Me too, Mr. Reigns, I'm so sorry. Are you like, okay?" asked Lori also hugging him.

"Yes, girls, I'm fine, I'm fine," he said holding Paige's hand. "I think I'd like a cranberry juice, lots of ice..."

"I know, a slice of lemon and a straw," said Lori already knowing how he liked his cranberry juice served, among other things.

"Would you like anything to eat?" asked Paige.

"No, not yet, what's on the menu for dinner?"

"We have two choices for you, I picked one and Lori picked the other. You can have filet mignon with balsamic syrup and goat cheese, roasted asparagus with tomato basil sauce, and as an appetizer fried shrimp with pureed mango dipping sauce and an oyster and corn chowder soup," Paige said smiling from ear to ear knowing that he would be pleased with her choice.

"And I picked for you pan sautéed red snapper with vanilla lemon butter cream, roasted zucchini with feta cheese and mint, summer pea mint soup, and your favorite pineapple casserole for dessert or the brandied peaches," said Lori as if her menu would knock Paige right out the box.

"I don't know which to choose, they both sound really delicious. You do this to me, every time," he said as the girls started giggling and bouncing around him as most women did.

"Okay, are you sure you don't want anything?" asked Paige.

"No, just the cranberry juice, maybe a cup of that oyster and corn chowder soup," he added winking at Paige.

"Okay, right away, Mr. Reigns," said Paige as she winked back at him and left immediately to fetch the cranberry juice as if her life depended on it.

"I'll help her," said Lori as she bent down and kissed his cheek, happy to see him again.

They landed safely at the Rafael Nunez International Airport in Cartagena, Columbia. A private car would be waiting for Dante, pre-arranged by Oso. It would take him to the city of Cartegena where Dante would meet with Oso and then the private car would bring him back. It was here where he said goodbye to his security detail.

"You sure you don't want me along for this ride. I got a bad feeling about this place," said Big Boom looking around at all the Columbians thinking of how violent and vicious they were.

"I'll call you, on my return back. Don't worry Big Boom. I'll be fine."

"Yes, sir, be careful, sir," said Big Boom.

"Always that," said Dante as he stepped foot off the plane, onto a portable stair landing and crossed the lot to where a private black on black Cadillac Escalade was waiting for him.

"Senor Reigns, vien, vien."

Big Boom watched as the men escorted Dante to the Escalade and closed the doors behind them. The Escalade made a u-turn and drove away. *I got a bad feeling about this,* Big Boom thought to himself.

The ride to Cartagena seemed to be longer than Dante expected. Then he realized he wasn't going to Cartagena at all. The sign on the side of the road read Cauca River twenty miles.

"Hola me disculpe, no es de Cartagena. Vamos por mal camino?" Dante said.

"No, esta es la manera correcta. Medellín es en la que están ordenados a hacer. Va a tomar un barco y viajar a través de las montañas por el río Cauca a Medellín. A continuación, se examinarán en la montaña a donde Oso le estará esperando," said an older Columbian man no more than five foot three inches tall, with the deepest, huskiest voice imaginable.

"El río Cauca es," said Dante wondering what in the world he had gotten himself into. He looked at his phone, no signal, no bars. He pressed for his walkie talkie, but it seemed to be out of range.

"The mountains, no phones, no lines," said the Columbian escort.

How will I call them, how will I tell them that they're taking me to Medellin? How will they know where I am? Dante began to feel uneasy and a bit nervous. He looked out the window of the Cadillac Escalade. *What part of the game is this?* This wasn't part of the plan. The plan was Cartagena, not Medellin.

Chapter Twenty Eight

Princess paced the floor as she periodically stopped and looked at Damian on the operating table through a glass observation window. The procedure would involve metal screws being placed into Damian's skull while electro-magnetic waves stimulate his brain cavity.

"Will he be...the same?" she asked frowning up her face as Dr. Holland explained all the scientific methods he planned to use to bring Damian out of his comatosed state.

"Well, I would hope so. We wouldn't want him to be any different now would we? Like a Dr. Jeykell and Mr. Hyde?" he laughed at her question unknowingly.

Laugh all you want, it better work or we'll see whose laughing when I'm done with you.

Just then her cell phone began to ring and an assistant of Dr. Holland's appeared in the doorway.

"I'm sorry ma'am all electronic devices must be turned off and stored away," a young man advised as if he were a flight attendant on an airline.

"Hi Princess, we'll be starting soon, so I just wanted to check in on you and make sure you were okay," said Daniella peeking through the doorway.

"Oh yeah, I'm fine, I'm just worried, what if it doesn't

150

work?"

"It has to work. It's what we do here at Bio One. Trust me, he'll be fine," said Daniella smiling from ear to ear. "Just think, in a few hours, he'll be awake, smiling, laughing and talking as if nothing ever happened," said Daniella as if Princess had no choice but to believe her.

"I hope so, Daniella. I hope so."

"Excuse me, Mr. Reigns has some visitors in the lobby."

"Who?" asked Princess wondering who would be there.

"It's a Ms. Moore and a Ms. Hess, ma'am."

Oh God, please don't tell me I have to sit in here with these two bitches.

"Fine, let them in," spat Princess as if the world was coming to an end.

"Oh, come on, can't be all that bad," smiled Daniella.

"You have no idea," said Princess as Stacia and Grace were directed into the room by the orderly.

"Hi Princess, I figured you'd be here. Where's Dante?" asked Grace.

"He's home, he's working, if you must know," said Princess wondering why Grace was worried about Dante.

"Just wondering," said Grace as she seated herself then pulled out her cell phone.

"No phones, no electronic equipment. Please turn all electronics off and store them away," smiled Daniella.

"I have to make an important call," said Grace.

"Checking in with the FBI are we?" added Princess.

"Yes, if you must know."

"Well, out the doors to the left is a waiting area where cell phone use is allowed."

"Thank you," snipped Grace as she rolled her eyes at Princess before walking out the door.

"Wow, you two sure know how to show the love," said Stacia.

Whatever, said Princess as she seated herself in the first row and looked at her brother lying on the operating table.

Please God just let him be alright.

Dante watched for signs of anything that would tell him where he was going. Unfortunately, there were none. The driver of the Escalade pulled over on the side of a dirt road.

"Esto es, el fin de la línea," Dante heard him say.

The doors to the Escalade opened and everyone seated began to unload.

"¿Dónde estamos nosotros? ¿Dónde vamos nosotros?" Dante asked.

"Paciencia, mi amigo, tenga por favor paciencia," said another one of the Columbian escorts.

Did he just call me friend? And tell me to be patient. I'm in the middle of a forest with mountains surrounding me and I have no idea where I'm going or what is going to happen to me and this guy wants me to be patient.

"Las manos, me dan sus manos," said the five foot three Columbian.

"¿Las manos, lo que para?" questioned Dante as he was approached from behind by two other Columbians. He quickly turned around to see them grabbing him.

"Suelte el jode de mí!" he yelled and screamed but the four man team quickly wrestled him to the ground and tied his hands behind his back then blindfolded him.

"Anda, permita que nosotros conseguirlo al río," Dante heard one of them say.

"Sí, el barco viene," said another.

A boat, a boat to where?

Dante yelled help in Spanish and English at the top of his lungs until he felt a blow to his stomach. It literally took the wind right out of him and his knees dropped to the ground as his arms crossed one another holding his stomach trying to catch back his breath.

"Nosotros no queremos dolerle. Acabamos de hacer nuestro trabajo. Coopere por favor con nosotros y será más fácil para usted." He could hear the voices talking as they picked him up off the ground.

"Permítanos ir, llevamos retraso. Nosotros no queremos decepcionar Oso."

Dante could feel himself being pushed along a dirt path. He could hear the sound of a flowing river not too far away.

"¡Pacho, aquí!" said the Columbian with the familiar voice.

"Fernando, tiempo largo no ve, ¿Dónde usted fue? Cómo sea su familia," said Pacho as he stood up, his arms opened wide.

"Mi familia es buena. He estado trabajando duramente" said Fernando as he embraced his older cousin. "¿Dónde está Vedo?"

"El se casó a Carmelita, él está en su luna de miel."

"Ninguna manera," said Fernando. "Carmelita es una mujer caliente que mira," he said joking and hugging his cousin.

"Aquí él es, Dante Reina. Una entrega especial para Oso," said Fernando as everyone laughed. "Tenga cuidado con él, él quizás trate de saltar el barco. Este de aquí nos ha estado dando mucho problema," said Fernando.

"Ah mi Dios, los caimanes comerán su asno vivo seguramente. Venga a mi amigo, antes que ellos le consigan," said Pacho as everyone laughed again. Dante could feel himself being walked into the water. "Anda, subida en el barco, lo ayuda en," said Pacho. "Muero de hambre. He estado en este barco fuera aquí en este río todo el día."

The Columbians shook hands and all embraced after

153

Dante was safely seated on the boat.

"Adiós Pacho," said Fernando as he and the other three Columbians watched Pacho start the engine to the boat and begin his take off as he yelled goodbye and waved to everyone.

"Diga bueno adiós, Dante Reina, salimos ahora."

"Jódale," he mumbled under the covering they had placed over his head.

Chapter Twenty Nine

The observation room had become somewhat over crowded to say the least. Grace and Lil Damian, Stacia Hess, Dajon, Antoinette, their two children, Princess, and even Uncle Deacon had all gathered together for the procedure on Damian.

Princess had balled up in the corner of a love seat, she opened her eyes, looked at her Vacheron Constantin. It was one twenty in the morning. Empty boxes of Chinese food, a suduko puzzle magazine and remnants of Dajon's children were scattered about the room.

You'd think they'd clean up after themselves. She said as she began to pick up the trash everyone left behind. Dajon was sleep on the other side of the room. *Everyone must have gone home,* Princess thought. She stared out the glass wall into the operating room. Damian's body still lay in a comatosed state. Princess looked at her watch again. *It's been seven hours since Dr. Holland started the procedure.* Princess began to feel that something was wrong, that the procedure wouldn't work. No matter what quacky Dr. Holland tried, her brother wasn't going to wake up. *It wasn't supposed to take this long, was it?* She asked herself before picking up her cell phone and walking down the hall to where cell phone use was allowed.

She turned on her phone, eight messages and twenty-seven missed calls. *Oh my God, what now?* It was like a sixth sense and she felt something was horribly wrong. She scanned the numbers through her phone. She dialed back to Brandon Reigns who was in charge of security along with his sister, Mina Reigns.

"Princess, where have you been, we've been trying to reach you?"

"I'm in the hospital. They're trying to bring Damian out of the coma, but nothing so far." She looked at her watch again, "Its one thirty in the morning what's the matter?" she asked yawning.

"Dante, he never came back, he never came back to Air Reigns One. The guys are still there, Big Boom said he's not coming back to Texas without him, dead or alive, they're all waiting at the airport."

"Didn't someone call him, ring his phone or send him a signal on the walkie talkie?"

"Of course, they're getting nothing. No response, no nothing."

"What the hell have they done to my brother?"

"I don't know, but Princess, Big Boom had unidentifiable security strategically awaiting Damian's arrival at the hotel in Cartagena and they claim he never showed and there's no sign of El Jeffe or his people either at the hotel."

"Oh my God," she said as she dropped the phone, her worse nightmares coming true. "Oh my God," she said as she covered her mouth, pulled back the tears and began to order Brandon on how to move forward.

"I'll make some calls and I'll call you back. Tell Big Boom I said not to leave my brother behind. He is to stay at the Cartagena Airport for the rest of his life until we find Dante, all of them," she ordered.

"Yes, Princess," said Brandon hanging up the phone and hoping for the security's sake that Dante showed up sooner rather than later.

Princess hung up the phone. She couldn't believe that Oso had turned on them, that Oso had taken her brother to do only God knows what to him, when it was the Reigns family that gave him his power. Had it not been for her brother and the death of El Jeffe, Oso would have no control. He would be nothing. *I can't believe...oh God please, not Dante. Please God don't let anything happen to him.*

She picked up the phone and dialed Dante's number. Big Boom was right, nothing it didn't even seem to dial, just went straight into his voice mail. She then began to place calls out to all the other states. Even though it was the middle of the night and most would be sleeping, there would be those that wouldn't be. Barry Groomes of Arkansas picked up on her third ring.

"Whose this?" he answered half sleep.

"Barry, it's me Princess. I'm so sorry to bother you, something drastic has come up and I desperately need to contact Oso, do you know how I can reach him?" she asked.

"Princess, it's the middle of the night. Do you think you can reach him tomorrow sometime?" asked Barry exhausted and desperately tired.

"No, Barry, please, I'm sorry to bother you, but this is rather urgent. I wouldn't ask if I didn't need this from you," she said knowing that he was ready to discontinue the call.

"It must be mighty important waking people up in the middle of the night like this. Gosh, Princess, I don't even think Oso was ever in my phone. I'm sure I can call around, someone has to have his number, but you're gonna have to give me until the morning. The only number I have is El Jeffe's. I guess I can go on ahead and erase that thanks to you guys," he joked to himself, Princess not finding the conversation to be a laughing matter at all.

"Barry, I need to reach Oso, it's a matter of life and death. I need you to call me back with his number as soon as you can?"

"Okay, Princess, hold your horses. You know if I say I'll do something, I will."

"Fine, Barry, tomorrow," said Princess as she hung up from him and tried placing some calls into the other states. She tried to call Juan Zapata who ran Arizona, Julian Jones out of Mississippi, Jamie Forrest of Tennessee and host of others, but no one answered. She left messages. By tomorrow she'd have Oso's number and she'd be able to make a call. If she didn't, she'd be on the next plane smoking, hunting down her brother and looking for answers. She'd be in Columbia by tomorrow night. No matter what it took, she'd track him down.

She went back into the observation. They were still operating. She placed her hand on Dajon's knee and rocked it gently calling his name.

"Yeah, yeah," he said, pushing her hand off of him.

"Dante is missing," she said softly leaning into his ear.

"What?" said Dajon coming to and realizing he wasn't dreaming, the voice was his sisters.

"I said Dante is missing. He went to Columbia to take a meeting with Oso, the one who took over the head of the Columbian Cartel after we murdered El Jeffe and he never came back to the plane. They're still at the airport waiting for him. The worse part is, no one can make contact with him, and he should have been back hours ago."

"What are we going to do?" asked Dajon ready to take action.

"What else can I do? I'm going to have to go to Cartagena, Columbia and find him or find Oso, but I can't just sit here in the Americas while Dante is missing."

"I'm going with you," said Dajon, sitting up ready to take action as if he were created by Marvel.

"Dajon, Columbia is a very dangerous place. The President has issued a travel advisory, Americans are kidnapped every day, I just don't know. The drugs and the cartels, it could be very dangerous, too dangerous for you," she said looking at him sideways, wondering if he really had what it takes after all these years.

Dajon wasn't a fighter like his brothers and Princess. He was more like...Ghandi, 'let's talk, let there be peace', that was Dajon. Dajon wasn't built for war, for controlling power, for running an empire. He lacked timing and instinct, everyone knew that.

"You're my sister and he's my brother, I should go with you," he said in a stern voice.

"I know Dajon and that's why I've always loved you, but really, I don't want you to go with me. It's not your place and just knowing that you would, is enough for me, enough for Dante. Do you understand, I need you here to take care of Damian and Angela," said Princess, smiling softly at him. "You're a good brother," then she kissed his cheek. "I love you."

"I love you, too and I'll stay. But, if you need me, Cartagena here I come!" he said confidant and strong.

They shared a laugh, just as Daniella and Dr. Holland, threw off their face masks and hugged one another, both leaning down onto Damian. Daniella kissing the top of his forehead, rubbing his arms as they gazed through the glass at everyone below astonishingly flabbergasted. Everyone in the room told Princess and Damian that Dr. Holland and Daniella had miraculously brought Damian out of his coma.

"Princess, look! It's Damian! Look, his eyes are open," said Dajon, completely pushing her body to the side so she could see.

"They are, they are," she said as people were moving in and out of an unrivaled view. It looked as if he was speaking. She stood up, Dajon along side her and they simultaneously moved toward the glass getting a better look at Damian lying below them, conscious, alert and appearing splendid.

"Oh Dajon, Damian's okay, he's okay!" Princess screamed excitedly.

She hugged Dajon as he tried to fight back his tears of joy for his brother. "I was scared for him," he confided in his sister.

"I know me too. Thank God for the doctor and Daniella. Can you imagine, thank God he's Bio One!" said Princess slapping a high five with her brother as if they were the Obamas.

Chapter Thirty

"¿Puede tomar usted esto de mi cabeza?" asked Dante tired of the head covering, wanting to take a deep breath of fresh air in, if only for a moment.

"¿Seguro, por qué no?" Pacho agreed. He untied a knot around Dante's neck and slid the pillow case covering from over his head. "¿Cómo es eso?"

"Gracias, mejor. Puedo respirar otra vez," said Dante happily as he began to breathe in deep breaths. "Los Wow miran su barco. Usted necesita una mejora mi amigo."

"Sí, ahorro para conseguir algo nuevo," said Pacho as Dante leaned back in the boat. The night air was so clean, so crisp. A warm breeze moved across the river, cricket sounds filled the air, and lightening bugs lit up like twinkle stars across the rivers edge and into the bush.

Pacho was humming a Spanish love song. He steered the tiny boat down the river as Dante kept a watchful eye, quietly untieing the rope that had his hands bound to one another behind his back. Just as the last loop was unknotting, Dante grabbed the rope with both hands and put it around Pachos neck, strangling him. But before he could jerk Pachos neck, Pacho elbowed Dante in his ribs, turned and punched Dante in the face, causing him to stumble and lose his balance. He fell into the Cauca River, back first.

Pacho turned the boat around frantically looking in the water where Dante fell in.

"Oye, Dante Reina, dónde está usted?" he yelled out into the dark, night sky.

Dante could hear the muffled sounds of Pacho calling out to him as he swam away from the boat. Less than twenty feet from land, an alligator emerged from behind him and began to swim in close, then another emerged from the river, and then another.

"Los Reinados de Dante miran detrás de usted, los caimanes le conseguirán," said Pacho, now steering his boat toward Dante and the alligators. "Usted necesita para esperar que yo le llegue a antes que ellos hagan, mi amigo."

Dante swam faster and faster as the alligators one by one closed in on him. He turned around to the alligator's mouth wide open, his teeth ferocious and his scaly greenish body horrifying. Dante closed his eyes anticipating his body being bitten in half.

"Oye, oye, oye," said Pacho, as he nudged Dante's shoulder. "usted bueno?" he said as he woke Dante up out of his sleep.

Dante wiped the side of his face as he opened his eyes to the rising of the sun across the Caucus River, the orange and red tones that danced on the moving water eased his beating heart.

"Sí, soy fino. Soñaba, los caimanes le conseguían y tuve que guardarle, Pacho," said Dante putting a look of certainty on his face.

"Son usted seguro porque la manera que usted chillaba para la ayuda, yo pienso que los caimanes quizás habían sido después de que usted," he said laughing at Dante and then mimicked him and began screaming for help like a girl. "La mirada, ellos le esperan,

Dante Reina," said Pacho as he pointed down the river.

"¿Dónde estamos nosotros?" Dante asked.

"Usted está aquí con Oso. Todo esto es Oso," said Pacho as he extended his arms looking up into the vast and bountiful mountains. "Esto es donde decimos nuestras despedidas," said Pacho smiling that they were there. "Soy muy hambriento, que tal usted."

"Sí, muriendo de hambre," smiled Dante back.

The boat ride had lasted all night, but he was safe. A long limousine was waiting and two husky body guards were standing on side the front and the back.

Dante sat down into the plush leather and was offered a glass of ice water by the man himself.

"How was your trip, Dante Reigns?" asked Oso.

"Well, let's just say, I hope you visit me next time," said Dante laughing and shaking hands with Oso.

Princess paced back and forth outside the recovery room that Damian had been transported to. She just wanted to see him and talk to him and know for certain that he was okay, no transformation, super hero, special powers or God forbid a complete foreign being.

The door opened and Daniella invited Princess inside.

"Here he is, Princess. Damian is back and doing better than ever," said Daniella.

"Oh my God Damian, are you okay?" said Princess as she ran over to his bedside leaning down on him, hugging him, and stroking the side of his bandaged head.

"I'm fine, I got a little headache, and I'm starving, but I'm fine. Where's Dante?"

She looked in her brother's eyes, he was Damian, it was him. No foreign being, no super hero, just Damian and she was so glad to see him.

"He left two days ago for Columbia for a meeting with

Oso and no one have heard from him. Damian, I'm going to Cartagena to bring him back, but first I don't know how to tell you this," said Princess with so much to tell. "Mother, she...mommy was killed." To say the words brought tears to her eyes. Damian looked at his sister wanting to pinch himself, he felt as if he was in a time machine and needed to find the time he had lost. Life moved without him and he missed the pieces.

"I don't understand?" said Damian.

"The night of your accident, a gang of thugs stormed the ranch. They shot everything up, everything. Dante wants the ranch demolished, completely. I was shot, everyone Damian, it was horrible. I had no time, no warning. They bum rushed the house and all I heard was automatic guns firing and everyone was screaming and I tried to protect her, but she was shot multiple times in the back, she died in the house. We had to have a funeral for her and everything without you because you were in a coma. We didn't know what to do."

"Mother is gone," said Damian already crying as he listened to his sister explain the death of their mother.

"Yes, and I miss her terribly," said Princess as she sat on the side of Damian's bed, handed him a tissue and looked quietly at a replica of Van Gogh's Sunflowers. "Sometimes, I wish I had the power of time. Just freeze it or stop it or even reverse it and change things. If I could, I would bring her back," said Princess.

"I know Princess, I know," said Damian patting her on the shoulder.

"I have better news though," said Princess smiling at him. "Probably the only news that could make you feel an inkling better," she said standing up.

"Your wife filed for divorce sighting irreconcilable differences and she's not seeking alimony or any spousal support or lawyer fees and she's not claiming any personal property or assets that you may have."

Damian smiled at his sister. He couldn't believe what she was saying. He had been asleep too long.

"I don't believe you. She would never in a million years divorce me, she wouldn't do it. I was her ticket to the Americas and to 'Ethiopian Princesses Gone Wild', no way Jose," said Damian dying to know how Princess accomplished that impossible task.

"You just remember you owe me one dear, sweet, brother," said Princess leaving out the little car bomb Patrick left in Dante's Fiorno that almost killed him.

"Yeah, your right, sis. I owe you big," said Damian.

"You bet a rat's ass you do. I really saved your life," said Princess convincing her self as well as him.

The limousine took the men to Oso's compound in the middle of nowhere except green acres of rolling fields and mountains. It was a picture perfect Juan Valdez back drop. Oso ordered his men to clean Dante up and even had clean clothes for him to change in. Servants moved around the compound that was complete with any and everything the imagination could think of. To be in the middle of absolutely no where, one must have everything one could possibly think of and so he did.

"This is some place you got here," said Dante as he walked two steps behind Oso down the marble hall over looking an indoor marble swimming pool surrounded by waterfalls, lush greenery and rock walls.

"Thank you, I'm glad you like it. You are welcome here anytime, Dante. Just tell your sister, Princess, she must play nice with me. I'm scared of her."

"So am I."

They both laughed as they entered a room, a large table with over twenty eight leather chairs seated around it.

And in one of the chairs it was none other than Don Vincente Pancrazio, tied up with a piece of electrical tape across his mouth.

"See, I figured that after everything has been said and everything has been done, I owe you at least one small favor," said Oso as he extended his arm and showed off the gift he had ascertained for Dante. "He's yours, you can do with him what you want, and then we can end this war, Dante. But, it ends with him, there can be no more blood shed. Do you understand my friend?"

Dante looked at Don Pancrazio. Then he looked back at Oso. He thought of his wife, Angela, his mother, and his brother. Everything that had been lost was so painful, he couldn't speak.

"I have my sources Dante, it is Don Pancrazio that started the war with you and your family after his brother was murdered. He is the beginning and he is the end. I brought him here, as a way of returning the favor to you," said Oso as he looked at Don Pancrazio whimpering and pleading under the tape on his mouth.

But we have much business to attend and the violence is just too much. Moving forward, we must be more vigilant, but more resilient to those we call our enemy, death is not the answer, it's only a never ending revenge," said Oso as he looked at Dante, "And your revenge is his much deserving death," finished Oso.

Dante just stared at the Don, he thought of a million ways he wanted to rip the flesh right off the Dons face, mutilate him, torture him and give him the slowest most painful death so that he'd be begging for mercy, but he turned his back to the Don, faced Oso and said, "Thank you, but killing him won't bring back my wife or my mother," said Dante.

Oso looked at him and smiled, was it his words that effected Dante Reigns, was it the war itself, the fight for power maybe had taken its toll. After fighting and winning and fighting and losing, you get to a point where you're tired of hitting, no matter how much you love the sport and Dante was at that point. He was tired of it all. He wanted something new for his life.

"If I can have one favor from you as a way of you saying thank you to me and my family, I don't want this piece of trash to be it," said Dante.

"Come, let's talk, you hungry?" asked Oso.

"Starving, I've been tied up in a tiny boat downstream all night, what do you think?"

Oso and Dante ordered lunch from an outside patio near the entrance to the foyer of his mansion. The compound was vast and unimaginable. Oso and Dante ate and talked as men, formulating and calculating the future. For Dante, he would walk away and never, ever look back. All his life, he had been under fire, but no more. He had built an empire with his brother and his sister, what did they need, nothing. And what did they want, nothing. There wasn't anything that they could not afford and now all they had was each other. His job was to over see his brother's legal businesses and operations, especially to oversee the business of Bio One Pharmaceuticals. The future was carved out for them, they would be legal drug dealers, offering over the counter medications and finding the cures to hundreds of ailments and illnesses. But, Princess had been fighting to gain the control ever since she had been stripped of her power and Damian had been assigned the head man in charge. Princess had been so determined to get her position back and still was. It was Dante's wish that Oso officially name her head of the Reigns Family Organization and pass to her sole and total control of the states that Damian currently controlled.

"Dante, are you sure this is what you want?"

"Yes," said Dante as if there was nothing else for Oso to possibly do.

"Well then, say it shall be and be it shall," he said as he handed Dante a pair of binoculars and pointed up at the sky at a helicopter hovering ahead.

Dante looked through the circle lens' to see Don Vincente Pancrazio's head busted open, blood pouring down his face and onto his torn suit jacket. Then suddenly with no warning, he was thrust from the open side door of the helicopter where he dangled in the sky from a rope around his neck.

"Where do you think Sosa learned such things from, my friend, huh, who?"

"You?" asked Dante arching his eyebrows up as horizontal lines creased across his forehead.

"That's right, Scarface baby!" said Oso holding up his hand to slap a high five with Dante. "Sosa is my middle name. Don't laugh, Dante, true story I tell you. You believe in me," he grinned from ear to ear.

"Always."

Chapter Thirty One

Oso and Dante ate, drank and took a walk through his massive 45,000 square foot compound. The day was coming to a close for Oso. He had to attend his daughter's ballet recital. God forbid he not be on time, he would never hear the end of it, from his daughter or her mother.

"Well, my friend, this is where we must say our good-byes," said Oso turning to Dante.

Dante stopped and looked at the sign that read 'Heliport Station'.

"Are you serious? You're putting me in the Sosa death-copter?"

"It's either that or Pacho and his little boat," laughed Oso. "Trust me, Dante, you will be in the safest of hands," said Oso as he turned to his guards. "No permítale suceder a este hombre!" he ordered as his guards bowed their heads one time.

"See, you are fine. Take the helicopter back to Cartagena. The mosquitoes will eat you alive out there on that river," said Oso.

After watching what they did to the Don when he took

his helicopter ride, Dante was weary to say the least. However, the river, Pacho and his boat and his group of cohorts were out of the question.

"The helicopter it is," said Dante not sure if he should be smiling at Oso or trying to snap the man's neck.

"Have a safe trip and I will take care of your sister, no worries, okay, Dante Reigns?" Oso asked shaking Dante's hand, then hugging him good-bye.

Princess left the hospital with a three man security team Brandon arranged for her. She had sat with Damian most of the day filling him in on everything that had happened since his accident. She had hoped to hear from Dante. But, they didn't. She went home, packed and was heading to the airport when the call came in. It was Dante. He had just made it back from the depths of the cocaine fields of Medellin, Columbia. He was in Cartagena and was safely boarding Air Reigns One.

"Dante, Dante, oh my God, where have you been? I was worried sick. Did they tell you, I chartered a private jet to fly to Cartagena? I was on my way to save you, literally."

"Princess, what could you have done to save me, do you know where I was? I was in the depths of the fields and on top of the mountains and I was tied up and put on a fishing boat and carried down stream, and I got attacked by alligators?" he said exaggerating.

"Well, why couldn't anyone reach you?"

"Didn't you just hear what I said Oso had me meet him at his compound in the mountains instead of the Sofitel Cartagena Santa Clara Hotel. And there's no phones, no reception. He had a special surprise for me waiting for me when I got there."

"What?"

"I'll tell you when I see you, but let's just say, the war is over," he smiled.

"Wonderful, that's wonderful, news. And guess what?"

"I already know, Damian is out of the coma, and he's okay. The machine that Dr. Holland and Daniella used on him, really worked, it's amazing isn't it. I really think this machine is going to bring Angela back too."

"That would be amazing, really Dante. I hope it brings her back."

"Have you grasped the concept that Bio One is going to make us richer than beyond our wildest dreams?"

"I honestly can't imagine," said Princess upset that he knew about Damian's successful procedure. "Who told you?"

"Security, who else, they were celebrating on our plane."

"I told them not to say a word."

"Don't' get mad. They have to tell me, Princess, who do you think runs things around here?"

"Me," she answered knowing that she did.

"I'll see you in a few hours. I'm boarding Air Reigns One," he said hanging up the phone on his sister as he walked up the stair rail and stepped inside the plane.

"Hi, Mr. Reigns, we were so worried about you. Thank God you're safe," said Lori her blonde, long hair bouncing around her face as she kissed Dante on his cheek and hugged him tightly.

"Thank you, Lori."

"Hi, Mr. Reigns," said Paige kissing the other side of his face."

"Hi Paige," he said hugging her as he kissed her cheek, then Lori's.

"I was so so worried, oh my God! We didn't know what happened to you. I'm just so glad you're safe."

"Oh my God, me too, Mr. Reigns, I'm just so glad your back safe and sound," said Paige rubbing his chest and leaning her head on him.

"Me too, I'm glad to see both of you, too," he said as

the girls went running off quickly and returning even quicker. Paige was holding his bottled VOSS water and a dish of lemons, while Lori had a glass of ice, and a straw.

"If you want anything Mr. Reigns, I'll get it for you," said Lori.

"Me too," said Paige, "Whatever you need."

"You girls are the best, I could use a massage. I had to sleep in a fishing boat. Can you imagine a fishing boat?"

"It must have been horrible for you, Mr. Reigns, you poor thing," said Lori, patting Dante's back. "I'll do it. I'll give you a massage."

"No, I'll do it," huffed Paige.

"Girls, how about you just take turns?"

"I'll go first."

"No me."

Princess continued to the airport, but instead of heroically saving her brother, her plan was to be there when his plane arrived and simply give him a ride home. *Home*, the thought went through her mind of her palatial estate outside of San Antonio, her condo downtown overlooking the city and the Reigns Family Ranch, which she had a financial vested interest along with her brother, Damian. Princess couldn't help but to think of their mother, Emory. The look on Damian's face was struck with grief and sadness when she told him the news. *He didn't even get a chance to say goodbye.*

Just then her phone rang, Princess answered on the third ring.

"Hello, Princess, how are you?"

She immediately recognized the voice on the other end and sent a chill through her. Flashes of their sexual escapades entered her mind.

"God, please, no," she screamed but it didn't matter.

Her screams only excited him and he'd kiss her mouth long enough to silence her, then suck the sides of her neck, her breasts, even her back would be marked by him.

"Oh, hi how are you?" she asked. "I wasn't expecting your call?"

His strength would hold her legs apart and his hands would squeeze her legs so hard he'd leave finger print bruises for days on her body.

"I heard what happened. I'm sorry about your mother," he said with sympathy for her and her family.

She could feel him next to her, breathing heavily into the side of her ear, digging into her body, thrusting in and out of her, throwing her up against walls, on top of dressers, and crashing onto her bed, their bodies holding onto one another for hours and hours and a time.

"What did you say?" asked Princess trying to concentrate on their conversation.

"I'm sorry about your mother, Princess. Really, if there's anything you need me to do, you know you got the whole state of Georgia riding with you baby," said Emil, his Southern charm reminding her of his bad boy ways. "How's Damian?" he quickly added.

"How'd you know about Damian?"

"I make it my business to keep my eye on you, pretty lady," said Emil. "That's what I do. You know how I do, Princess. You already know. Stop acting like you don't."

Princess couldn't help but to smile. She did know him too. As sadistic as she was, he was probably the best match for her and deep down inside, that Emil was always there for her, even when he was miles away in Atlanta, Georgia.

"I know exactly what you do," she said in her sexy, 'come fuck me right now' voice. "The problem is, you do it a thousand miles away with a thousand other people," she added with a hint of jealousy amongst her sarcasm.

"Let me find out you got some jealous bones for me

hiding in your closet, Princess," he said smiling as he looked at himself in the mirror.

"I got something for you but it's not bones," she said smiling back as she entered into the private passenger parking area of the airport.

"You know what, that's it. I'm going to the heliport right now. I want to see what you got for me when I get there," he said making a u-turn, dead serious and on his way to the heliport where his private helicopter would be ready and waiting.

"Let me get off this phone with you, and find me a pilot right quick. I'm coming to San Antonio, tonight."

"Goody," she said thinking of all the things he would do to her once he got there.

"You ready for me?"

"No, but I will be by the time you get here," she said hanging up the call.

She parked her car and stepped out just in time to watch Air Reigns One land safely. The hatch opened as the ground crew placed a portable stair case by the door and Princess watched as Dante emerged looking like a million bucks and then some. He walked down the flight of steps, safely touched ground and kissed his sister's cheek.

"Wow, you look fabulous?" said Dante.

"Yeah, hot date," she said looking seductively devilish.

"I'm scared to ask."

"Emil," she said as they walked over to her Aston Martin DB9.

"He's flying in?"

"Yeah, yeah, he said he's on his way," she said watching her brother trying to detect concern.

"Emil's a great guy. I think you two make a perfect match," said Dante pleased that Emil made the call as he had instructed him. God knows if Princess was about to be the head of the Reigns family empire, Dante would need someone he could trust close to her.

"Don't try to match my maker, brother dearest," said Princess.

Dante just looked at her wondering if she had any idea he was playing cupid.

"Take me to Damian."

Princess looked at him, frowning and staring at him like he was crazy.

"Please," he added just in the nick of time.

Princess started the car and left the private passenger parking. She had three Suburbans along for the ride with two man teams inside of each. There were two Suburbans behind them and one in front of them. She rang into the driver of the car in front of them. "Our destination is Bio One."

Dante walked into the massive stone building and headed to the recovery station where Damian's room was located.

He opened the door to find his brother awake, laughing and in high spirits.

"Damian," said Dante as he walked over to the hospital bed, bent down and hugged his older brother.

"Thank God your safe, Dante. We were worried sick," said Damian.

Dante heard his brother's voice and smiled at him. "No thank God your weird and you keep all these weirdo scientific specialists around and they brought you back," said Dante teasing his brother as always.

"Hi Dante," smiled Stacia.

"Stacia, look whose here? Wow, it's everyone," he said spotting Grace in the room as well. "No sewers are safe with you Grace," Dante said joking thinking about the two of them wrestling out on the Reigns Ranch lawn.

"Hello, Dante, it's so good you're home and safe and sound," said Anjoinette, hugging him and kissing him on the left cheek then the right.

"Yes, good to see you to, always good to see you," he said embracing her and then his brother, Dajon.

"Good to have you back, Dante," Dajon said letting his brother go.

"Yeah, it feels good. I'm just glad Damian is okay," he said play punching Damian's arm. "I got a lot to talk to you about," Dante smiled.

"It's all good I hope."

"Good indeed, no hope needed, brother," he said as he looked at Grace.

Just then the door to the recovery station room opened and an out of breath, sweaty, and shaking Daniella burst into the room.

"Damian, it came! It came! The FDA approval of RD-221 and RDX-214, it passed," she said running over to his bed side, letter in hand as she held it for him to read.

"Do you know what this means?" she asked him, "Do you know how big this is, Damian?"

"It's my dream, Daniella. Oh my God, thank you," he said as he grabbed her face with both his hands and gave her what started out to be just a simple kiss on the lips but Daniella took full advantage of the opportunity and parted her lips sucking him in.

"Wow, now you don't see that every day," said Princess as she watched her brother let Daniella go, realizing that the entire room was watching.

"It passed, guys our drugs passed. We now hold the cure for AIDS and the cure for cancer in our hands," he said completely dumbfounded and out of breath from kissing Daniella. "You're amazing," he said staring in her eyes knowing that none of this would be possible without her. His even being there right now was because of her and Dr. Holland.

"No, really, you're amazing," Daniella replied her heart pounding wishing they were completely alone at that very moment.

Stacia and Grace simply looked at one another both a little unraveled and on edge with the Daniella girl that Damian kept referring to as 'we' and 'us'.

Daniella looked down at her blackberry and read out loud a text message she had just received from Bio One's Cherin King who was Damian's lawyer. "It's confirmed, Good Morning America, CBS News with Katie Curic and the Oprah Winfrey show. They all want to interview you! Can you believe it? This is fabulous news, Damian, simply fabulous!"

"The Oprah show? Are you kidding me? This is fantastic!" yelled Damian holding up his fist and giving Daniella a pound as he hugged her and began kissing her once again. He was most happy at that moment than he had ever been in all his life. Everything he was would now stand for something of great magnitude and everything he'd worked for, would be for the world to see.

Dante's cell phone rang as the room exploded in cheer. "Get some bubbly," ordered Dajon as he spoke to security standing vigil outside the room. "And some glasses," he hollered out the door.

"Yes, sir, right away, sir," the security guard hollered back.

As the jubilee of Damian's Bio One's star achievements filled the room Damian stopped smiling as he watched his brother take a call. He could tell that something was terribly wrong.

"I'm on my way. I'll be right there."

"What's happened?"

"It's Angela Dr. Bailey said that she's gone into premature labor. He said her body has begun to release poisonous toxins that are harmful to the baby. He said he thinks he's going to have to perform an emergency C-section.

"Oh, Dante, no...you must hurry," said Anjoinette knowing that Angela was only in her seventh month. She crossed her heart, the born-bread Catholic that she was.

"Yes, hurry, Dante," said Damian. "We'll get Dr. Holland and send him over," Dante quickly added as if Dr. Holland was life's greatest hope. "Take care of my brother and my brother's wife," he ordered Daniella.

"Of course I will. I'll call Dr. Holland right away," she said as she looked at Dante and Princess. "Come, we must hurry," said Daniella as she led Princess and Dante out of the room.

"Don't worry I'll get you there, Dante," said Princess grabbing Dante's arm.

Chapter Thirty Two

As Princess pulled her DB9 into the cul de sac of the hospital's entrance, Dante hopped out the sports car as Daniella hopped out of the Suburban in back of them. She had been riding with a four man security detail following closely behind the DB9.

"This way, Daniella," said Dante as they ran down the hall, taking the elevators up to her floor, where a nurse working on some medical charts at the nurse's station saw them running past her. She recognized Mr. Reigns on sight.

"She's downstairs on four, they're prepping her for surgery," said the nurse as Daniella and Dante took off for the stair case to the fourth floor.

As a security guard opened the door to the fourth floor, another one held it open for security, Dante and Daniella to go through first. They ran over to another station where two women were seated. One was on the phone the other looked up at Dante's frantic face and calmly asked, "How may I help you?"

"I'm looking for my wife, Angela Reigns, they said she's

on four being prepped for surgery."

"I will check on her for you sir, right away. If you like you can step into the waiting room and have a seat. I'll only be a couple of minutes," said the on-call receptionist filling in on the surgery floor.

Within less than two minutes she was standing in the waiting area, "Excuse me, Mr. Reigns, you may come with me," she said taking him across the floor and into another tiny small private waiting room. "Your wife is in surgery, sir, but you and your family and friends will be accommodated in the President's Wait Lounge. It was much nicer and more accommodating than the regular waiting area. There was a fully stocked bar, a fully stocked refrigerator, dishes and silverware, the hospital room service menu which featured a fine dining selection and a flat screen on the wall, remote control, four sofas, three loveseats and plenty of tables and chairs.

"I'm Dr. Daniella Worthington. I'd like to prep and assist Dr. Bailey, may you please make that request immediately," ordered Daniella already knowing that Damian would want her to oversee Dr. Bailey and the hospital staff, and possibly even assist. And what Damian wanted, Damian got.

"Well...I don't know are you a doctor here?" asked the on-call unfamiliar with the doctors on that floor.

"No, she's a Reigns family member and I want her with my wife. So, please, just make the request to Dr. Bailey, now," said Dante as if her life depended on it.

"Yes, sir, no problem," said the woman as she scurried away quickly.

"I think you scared her," said Daniella.

"I didn't mean to. I really didn't." Dante looked at Daniella with tears in his eyes. She could sense he was scared for Angela and she could feel his pain. She could see the love he had for his wife and she knew Dante didn't want to lose her. Damian had told her months ago all about his brother's wife, it was after all, her goal to bring Angela back using Dr. Holland's miraculous treatment. For Daniella, it was a classic love story and her honor, no her duty for the love of Damian to bring his brother's wife back to him. What more could she do to show Damian she cared.

"I just don't want anything to happen to her," he said sitting down in the chair, as the on-call came back as she promised.

"You may come with me, Dr. Worthington," said the on-call, looking at the big brawly security man, standing post at the door.

"Dante, don't worry, everything will be fine. I won't let anything happen to her, okay," she said hugging him closely and rubbing his back. "Relax, I'll come out and I'll keep you posted as often as I can," said Daniella smiling at Dante holding her thumb up in the air as the door began to close, but suddenly opened back up as Princess rushed inside the room and hugged her brother.

"Have they said anything?"

"No, Daniella just went inside with Dr. Bailey," said Dante as he stood up, and paced around the back of the chair, then sat back down.

Dajon and Antoinette walked through the door, the receptionist held for them. Antoinette hugged him and held his hand, while sitting next to him. Princess knew they were friends, but didn't understand the depth. It was Antoinette who had undying loyalty to Dante. *I wonder what's between the two of them?* But, what Princess didn't know was that Dante Reigns had saved her, saved her life and the lives of her children. Now, today, she had a loving husband and her life was full of riches beyond her wildest dreams.

It would be another two hours before the on-call would come to the room, "Excuse me, Mr. Reigns, there's a call for you at the front station."

Dante looked around the room wondering who it could be. He slowly stood up and walked toward the door, his heart beginning to pound. Daniella was waiting for him at the desk. "Come with me, Dante." She ushered him into a room, where he changed into scrubs and then was walked into a room where the doctors were hovering over Angela.

"I'm so sorry, Dante. They did everything they could, everything to keep her alive. But, she wanted to go."

Her words cracked into him, but his pain was covered by the mask he was told to wear.

Angela is gone? He couldn't think of a tomorrow without her being there. And as he walked over to where her body was laying on the operating table, he knew that if tomorrow came, nothing for him would ever be the same. *I love you,* he said as he saw her lifeless face, bending over the table and clutching her in his arms. *What will I do now, without you?* He couldn't think or talk. He couldn't hear anyone around him and the room went blank and all he could hear was his heartbeat. And then he whispered in her ear. "I wish it had been me in that car. I would die for you, Angela. I would give my life for you. I love you. I'll miss you every day I breathe on this earth without you." He deeply inhaled and filled his lungs with air, fighting back tears and the thoughts of losing Angela, his true life soul mate. "I will find you again, Ange, just wait for me, I will find you, I will find you," he said as he let her go, gently laying her body down.

Daniella moved in front of him, "Dante, please, I know this hard, I know it is, but I want you to look, for just one minute," said Daniella as she pointed twenty feet away through a glass windowed wall. At first he didn't see anything while zooming in on the doctor's working ferociously to stabilize the tiny 2lb 2ounce new born baby that they had delivered from Angela right before she died.

"She wouldn't let go, do you understand? Angela wouldn't let go until she got that baby here. She's an amazing woman and the baby is beautiful. Dante she's so beautiful," cried Daniella unable to hold back her tears as she looked at the teeny tiny baby fighting for her life. "Do you understand, I held her and I wrapped her and they took her because she can't breath yet, Dante, her lungs aren't developed, but once they get her incubated, she will be fine, just fine," said Daniella as she could see the tears in Dante's eyes and the smile under his mask.

She, thought Dante not believing that tiny two pound, eight inch-long baby, was his little, tiny, daughter. Her eyes closed shut, he saw her face when a doctor stepped to the side and just for that one moment he saw a piece of himself, and he saw a piece of Angela.

Don't worry Angela, I'll take care of her, said Dante looking through the windowed glass at the baby knowing that God did do things for strange reasons and there was reason in Angela's death, just as there was reason in his daughter's life.

"I held her, and I felt her, and she's a fighter, she's not going anywhere, so don't be afraid of her, she's stronger than I am," said Daniella her tears of joy for the baby sweeping under her mask as she looked up at Dante.

"Thank you, Daniella, for everything. I see why my brother's head over heels for you," said Dante.

Daniella still in tears now had a bigger smile on her face than Dante.

"Yeah, I better get back and check on him and let him know what's going on, will you be okay?"

"Yeah, I think I'll be fine," he said pulling it all together.

"Do you want me to let everyone know what's going on with Angela and the baby?" asked Daniella able to relive him.

"No, no, I got it, I can handle it. It is okay, it's all going to be okay. It's turning out for us how it's written for us to be," said Dante. "It's actually written perfect."

The End

TERI WOODS

PRESENTS

DEADLY REIGNS

III

THE THIRD OF A TRILOGY

Three Months, Five days, and eight hours later...

"You guys are really the best. No really, you didn't have to come all the way down here. Did they Lucky?" asked Dante as he bent down and kissed his tiny baby girl. Dante held the tiny bundled present from his wife as he walked down the hallway of the hospital. It was time to go home.

"Are you nuts? Of course we did. I'm a proud auntie to a niecey, finally!" Princess said sucking her teeth at Damian and his fleet of bad boys. "And Auntie Princey is going to take perfect care of that sweet little Lucky Reigns so help me God," screamed Princess as she cootchie cooed her niece. Damian was following closely behind as he slowly but surely made his way down the hall walking on crutches.

"Damian, you look like you need a wheel chair," noted Dante. "Seriously, Princess, do you see what you did to the man trying to blow up my car? I hope you learned a valuable lesson, that car bombs are not cool," said Dante shaking his head no at her. "People can get really hurt," said Dante as if a host on a talk show.

"Wait...what did you just say?" Damian asked as he quickly looked at Princess who was trying to silence Dante with her pointer finger up at her lips.

"See, you're always starting something, Dante, always," spat Princess before turning to Damian. "I'm so sorry, brother. It'll never happen again," she said smiling and rubbing his back.

"Don't touch me right now, really. I can't believe you."

And of course, they argued all the way home.

The End, Really

Coming Soon for

2010

Circle of Sins

For Gangsters Only

Confidential Informants

Beat the Cross

TERI WOODS

PRESENTS

Circle

Of

Sins

BY NURIT FOLKES

Chapter I

Rehashing the Past

The drive to Morganville, New Jersey was short but undeniably, sweet. The vehicle's effortless purring was overpowered by cackling, airy giggles and humorous yammering. Andre could only watch the backs of the heads of two attractive people seated in front of him. Their movements conjured visions of bobble heads and he smiled to himself. He then turned his attention to the adorable bundled up bundle of joy cooing in the inverted infant car seat, facing the Corinthian leather seats of Shawn's immaculate, freshly scented, Escalade.

Natalia's plans to fly off to the Virgin Islands after she assumed Shawn hated her guts were thwarted —to her and Andre's delight. Thankfully her assumptions were inaccurate since she was sitting next to her husband gazing into his slanted brown eyes, wondering what in the world did she do to deserve his dedication. She had sinned against this man in the worst way yet he found it in his heart to forgive her.

Shawn had since moved back to New York in hopes to

190

change his life for good this time. Although he didn't plan on staying in New York long and contracted private builders to start construction in New Jersey on a complex architectural structure that would blow the one he built in Atlanta out of the water. When he pulled up in front of the 23 acres of excavated property, Natalia's eyes widened as a subtle gasp escaped her slightly parted lips.

"Daddy, is that all ours?" she asked, still gazing out the window at the sea of struggling green grass bombarded with brown weeds dominating its vastness spreading out for miles under a pastel blue sky.

"Not really all ours," he took a daunting breath before filling her in, "I've got some other investors going in with me and we're not just building residences this time. We're going all out. We're building a mall and not just any mall. This is going to be one of the tallest malls around!"

Natalia finally turned to catch the enthusiastic grin plastered on the bottom half of her husband's handsome face and it reminded her why she'd fallen so hard for him. The splendid combination of one part tenacity, two parts ambition drenched with tons of confidence made up the enigma she affectionately dubbed, daddy. She admired him as he appeared entrenched in his own thoughts of grandeur and sighed, "God how I love you." He palmed the side of her delicate face and moved in ever so slow to kiss her.

"WAAAAAAAAH!" Baby Everton ruined the moment with an alarming wail. This siren-like noise jarred poor Andre out of his serene dream world where his man, Adonis bathed him in a creamy bath of silky milk.

"What in the hell?" Andre shot up from his cramped position and tended to his Godchild. "What's wrong with mommy's baby? Are you after mommy's boobies again?" Natalia, cooed in her baby's direction as Andre freed Everton from his car seat shackles. After pulling him out of the seat, Andre swaddled him tightly then passed him to his lactating

191

mother. Shawn's eyes followed the bundle to its final destination right under Natalia's melons. Everton eagerly latched onto his mother's supple taupe
nipple after she popped it out of her tank top and nursing bra.

"See? That ain't fair man," Shawn playfully palmed the infant's curly haired noggin and chuckled, "You know those nips used to be mine, lil' man?" Then he sighed, the kind of sigh that if it were translatable would mean: *What if this little motherfucker ain't even mine?* Shawn still struggled with the whole paternity issue. After all the infidelity between them, he was surprised to find that he really still loved his wife despite the fact that she had sex with his best friend, his brother and a secretly suspected unknown third man whom he fought desperately against grilling her about. He definitely wasn't a Saint and he kept that in mind every time second thoughts about making up with her plagued him. Subconsciously he feared that her being the cause of him murdering his best friend would ruin their future happiness some day. This secret he planned to take to his grave for sure.

"Damn, save some for me," Shawn joked as he watched Everton's tiny pursed lips devour Natalia's nipple in one motion. His tiny mouth puckered, retracting with precision. Natalia looked up at Shawn and smiled mischievously as thoughts of Shawn suckling on her gorged breasts enticed her. But in the back of her mind she knew it would be a little while longer before they'd be able to do the nasty. She had a lot of healing to do— mentally as well as physically. She was still dealing with the backlash from all of the idiotic decisions she'd made thus far. She wished she had done things differently after finding out about Shawn's extracurricular activities with countless women including her once believed best friend, Talea. As the name popped into her head she regretted what she set into motion, robbing Talea of her beauty by hiring a thug to slash it away. Now Talea would never model or act ever again with her newly carved out face. Natalia was ashamed of how she let her anger control her. This secret she would carry to her grave.

ക്രൈ

It never ceased to amaze Shawn how wonderful his wife was with Everton. She was a devoted, doting mother who managed to clean house, cook dinner and tend to him at night whereas Shawn tried desperately to carryout his secret agenda—getting Natalia pregnant. This time he'd know for sure if the baby was his. Regrettably, Everton was Natalia's baby and still his maybe.

Tonight she looked ripe in her booty shorts and tight t-shirt. Milk does the body good, well breast milk that is. Since Natalia breast fed Everton her stomach was flat again, curves formed in the right places and her already bodacious boobs were even fuller. Shawn watched as she leaned over Everton's crib, attentively, adoringly. Her back arched, ass poked out and he wanted to spank her in more ways than one. He inched up behind her, palmed her plumpness and whispered, "Daddy's home."

"Shhhh," she simpered and led him out of the newly furnished nursery in their upscale duplex. Shawn hated having to stay there but Natalia convinced him it made more sense for now rather than live out of hotels until their new home in New Jersey was fully complete.

"You are so naughty," she grinned, knowingly. She had been ready for some of Shawn's hot sticky pounding ever since she conked out on him the night before. Their passion had returned with a vengeance. It was as it used to be back when they made love for the first time. Shawn's stamina was back once he cut out all the drinking. They were serious about making the marriage work now and forever. She pulled him to her, slid her arms around his neck and they kissed like there was no baby and like they were the last people on earth. In between Natalia's legs were on fire, oozing readiness and Shawn's loins were ablaze, his tool handy, preparing for a momentous eruption. Shawn grabbed her buttocks and lifted her from the parquet floor. She clamped her toned legs around him as their kiss approached crescendo. He carried her out to the spiral staircase, pressed her curved back up against its supporting beam. He groped her feverishly as they panted loudly until he couldn't wait to be inside her. Shawn lowered her smooth legs until her feet touched the floor. He slowly undressed her enjoying the view with each revealing tug. His eyes remained glued to her supple mounds of female fat for a brief moment then he tossed her clothing. When she stood before him in her birthday suit he all but tore off his shirt. He hastily unbuckled his jeans and let them drop to the floor. Natalia knelt before him and was just about to give him the blow job of the century when her cell phone rang, the vibration forcing the glass coffee table to tremble. She was distracted for a bit but decided against answering it. She tugged and pulled until his boxer briefs were off and she was face to face with his sexy, thick magic stick. She massaged it up and down then in and out of her warm mouth as Shawn adored her from his imagined celestial view. Again the moment was interrupted by her phone. He was ready to throw the phone out the window now. He calmly excused himself from her taut mouth's powerful suction and picked up the cell phone, putting the call on speaker phone for his wife to answer it.

"Hello?" Natalia called out as she approached Shawn about to take the phone from his hand.

"Hello gorgeous," Seth, chimed. Seth's timing was the worst and Natalia could've died at that moment from fear of her husband misconstruing the call.

194

"Seth? Wh-why are you calling me?"

"Well, I'm in New York and I was wondering if I can take you out tonight."

"What? I haven't spoken to you in ages! And what the hell...you know I'm—"

"You gon' take me too, motherfucker?" Shawn growled.

"What? Who is that?"

"Don't worry about it nigga. Just tell me if you' gonna take me out too when you take my wife out."

"Uh, well, I didn't mean—I apologize," Seth stumbled and hung up abruptly.

"Who the fuck is that bitch ass nigga?" Shawn asked, while getting dressed.

"He's—"

"He's another nigga that fucked my wife, right?" Shawn spat and stormed out of the room.

Natalia ran after him and grabbed a hold of his arm. Shawn snatched his arm away from her, slamming the bedroom door in her face. Natalia slammed the side of her body into the door forcing it into Shawn's body. Shawn threw open the door and grabbed her by her shoulders. His stare cold. Natalia nervously and softly uttered, "I'm sorry. I was only trying to open the door..."

Shawn could see her fear and realized that she was actually afraid of him. He wasn't going to harm his wife but he was going to get to the bottom of the story behind the strange man calling her now, after all the promises they'd made to one another.

"B.G. you know I will never hurt you again. Don't act like you're afraid of me cuz that shit bothers me. You know I won't hurt you don't you?" he asked, releasing his grip on her shoulders and backing away. She seemed to be relieved now and she walked over to him, slipped her small hands around his waist and laid her head on his well developed chest.

"Yes, daddy, I know."

Shawn gently pushed her away looking deep into her eyes.

"Who is Seth?" The look of panic that flashed across her face said it all. Shawn now had an inclining of what he was about to hear. It was something he'd come to dread. Finding out that his once perfect wife was not all she was cracked up to be. The naive, conservative woman who seemed to have it all together was actually a perfectly disguised disaster. His hand swooped over his face and rested at his chin for a brief moment before dropping to his side. Natalia's eyes saddened and she began almost in a whisper, "I met him before I met you and when—

"I can't hear you. Speak up," Shawn commanded.

Natalia took a deep breath and adding little volume to her tone, "Wh-when we um, were going through our problems..."

Shawn let out an exasperated sigh and walked over to the bed and slowly lowered himself onto the edge of it,

"And?" he inquired, and leaned forward with his elbows resting on his knees. He couldn't look at her. He didn't really want to hear any more yet his mind raced and all kinds of questions gnawed at him, he felt inclined to get the rest of the story. Natalia came over, knelt down in front of him taking his hands into hers,

"You have to understand something," she paused to choose her words carefully, "I wasn't just out there. I've never been involved with different men like that before. I mean, somehow it was as if I could do the things that I've always thought were wrong. I was always doing the right thing and regarding myself so highly that I barely dated before Mark. I only had two sexual partners before Mark and I guess I felt cheated of the many experiences I've missed. I was always being the good girl yet people were hurting me constantly... like Tracy and Mark having sex. I mean there they were having sex behind my back and he got her pregnant. My husband got my best friend pregnant! Then there was all of you're cheating—"

"So I'm the reason you became a hoe?"

Natalia dropped his hands and stood up, "That's uncalled for. So is this how it's going to be? You're never gonna let me live it down or forget?"

"How can I, B.G.? Everton might not be my son. How do you expect me to feel now especially since I'm finding out that there's another nigga that could be his father?!? This shit is crazy!"

Shawn jumped up and got dressed then left the condo in a huff. Natalia didn't go after him this time. He called her out of her name for the last time. She truly felt that she wasn't a ho. She knew in her heart that she was not built like that. Admittedly, revenge and curiosity fueled her sexual trysts with three different men. But she accepted responsibility for her misjudgment of choosing her husband's best friend and his only brother as sex partners. Now that she'd made such grandiose mistakes she realized that there was no turning back. Shawn would either be stronger than most men and deal with it or end what she wanted most in life right now— their marriage.

੶ઝৎ

Shawn caught the elevator down as he cursed himself for allowing Natalia to convince him to rent the most expensive suite available. It was their home away from their brand new house on a secluded hill top property in New Jersey practically overlooking his proposed mall site. The apartment was amidst Manhattan's elite but was a major inconvenience for Shawn since he wasn't used to being surrounded by so many blue bloods. His bourgeoisie neighbors always made it a point to remind him of how unwelcome his 'kind' was in their presence. Although, his wife reveled in the duplex apartment's expansive opulence he was unimpressed. They both had money now and although Shawn's net worth couldn't put a dent in Natalia's, he could keep up with the Jones' and afford to take care of his high maintenance princess. He bought a bevy of expensive trinkets to make up for their past tribulations including his extramarital dalliances which caused Natalia so much grief. They were starting anew and Shawn was serious about the changes they both agreed on making and accepting. But now he wondered if he would ever be able to get past *the past,* especially now when it was resurfacing with a vengeance. Would he forever be reminded that his wife had turned into a whore no matter how brief? He kept imagining her with Maleek. He fought visions of his brother pumping into her and was thankful he didn't know what this new guy Seth looked like. He believed that she wasn't still seeing Seth but it was just too much for his pride never mind his ego. He sat in his car seething over everything. Then as if a swarm of calm encircled him, he realized the one constant that made his forgiveness take precedence over all the cons concerning Natalia. He *really* loved his wife. No ifs ands or maybes, there was no way he could fight it, she had his heart in a choke hold. He believed that he was mature enough, strong enough to withstand their issues. He believed that their love had beat the odds already so why not this? He got out of his S.U.V., went back upstairs to his wife and they hashed and re-hashed until there was a mutual understanding between them. After making up verbally their bodies made up, incessantly. He made love to her like only he could in order to convince himself that he was still the alpha male and to mark his territory so that his wife would never forget it.

৵৵৶

"It is unfortunate that we have to tell you this Mrs. Bryant but the term life insurance policy you're husband purchased lapsed," an insurance representative informed Maleek's widow.

"And? What the hell does that mean to me?" Faye angrily spat into the phone.

"Well, the two million dollar policy lapsed in the first year so we cannot disburse funds on that policy but the first –to-die permanent policy was paid up and we will be able to get the $250,000 dollar check out to you pending our internal to authorities' investigation comparative."

"So you're saying the main policy we paid up for a year doesn't exist? So what happened to all the money paid into it?"

"Mr. Bryant defaulted on the policy when he failed to make the monthly premiums even during the allotted grace period. It's not a universal policy which accrues cash value so it was simply canceled once it lapsed. This is all standard ma'am."

"So when will I get the check from the other policy?"

"It can range anywhere from 10 days to 3 months."

"3 months? What the hell...? I waited almost a year to hear this shit? I was told I would receive a check a month ago. Now I'm being told 3 months? I had to pay out of my pocket for my husband's funeral. As if I don't have enough to deal with now I find out I'm only collecting on one policy nearly a year later?!? That's crazy! Just send the damn check as soon as possible!"

Faye sucked her teeth and threw the phone down. She began sobbing and Fayette ran over to her bereaved mother and tried feeding her the half eaten chocolate chip cookie she'd been nibbling on for the past five minutes. Faye tried desperately to crack a smile as she obliged her daughter's kindness. Her teeth barely chipped an edge of the chocolate confection. She kissed Fayette's wrinkled brow and said, "Thank you baby."

"Your melcum mommy. Why you kwying mommy?" her adorable lisp, was music to Faye's ear at that moment, soothing her, pulled her away from the morbid thoughts of her deceased husband.

"It's okay, baby, mommy's going to be okay." Faye lied. The emptiness in her heart plagued her from dusk till dawn. Maleek was really gone. She still hadn't accepted it and unconsciously awaited his homecoming. The Dora the Explora theme song sounded from Fayette's bedroom so she abandoned her mother for her daily Dora fix.

Alone standing next to a vaccum cleaner, Faye unraveled its cord as she embarked on her cleaning ritual. She was stuck in her usual routine and often tried to pretend that her husband's death was a nightmare she could wake up from. Since her sons were with her sister at the mall at Peach Tree Center she knew they weren't coming home anytime soon. She relished the quiet whilst her rambunctious boys were away. Fayette was no problem and was quite independent just like her mother. Faye schlepped around the house cleaning relentlessly until she passed the door to Maleek's den. She palmed the door and felt a rush of emotions swell in her chest. She hadn't been in the den since the last of Maleek's personal belongings like clothes, electronic gadgets and papers were packed into boxes and neatly stacked in it. But today, a force of some kind beckoned her to the room. Today, she would go through his things, salvage mementos for the children but discard the rest. Her hand trembled as she turned the knob to enter. She could've sworn an icy breeze blew against her face as the door eased open. *Oh, it's just the AC on full blast in here, she nervously assured herself.*

The first box she opened was full of his prized

basketball jerseys. She knew that her sons wouldn't want to part with these treasures. She re-taped the box and moved onto the next box, she rummaged through DVDs, computer software even a barrage of cell phone accessories. She grabbed a bunch of the DVD cases and one fell from her hand, hit the side of the box and aptly landed in her lap. She reached for it and noticed two yellow post-its were stuck to it. The top post-it had her name written in Maleek's handwriting as clear as day. Faye's heart nearly jumped from her chest. Each breath became shallower as she inhaled and she realized that she had to calm down to keep from passing out. Eerily enough, she flipped over the DVD and read the title, "Fahrenheit 911" and she shook her head in amazement. She lifted the post-it with her name and read the second one: *MY WARRIOR PRINCESS, IN CASE OF AN EMERGENCY, TEXT THIS MESSAGE, MB119 TO PB'S CELL.*

Faye exhaled and placed her hand over the words. Her husband was communicating with her after his death and it didn't frighten her, it saddened her. It was then that she realized her husband would've wanted her to exude strength, handle her biz and get on with life. She remembered how he always referred to her as his next in command. He believed in her as she in him. Now he saw to it that she could get the much needed help she needed ever since their legal money in the bank accounts had dwindled considerably. She knew what to do and wasted no time. She sent a text to Shawn's cell with the special coded message and awaited his reply.

∞

Shawn's Side Kick cranked out a snippet of a Southern Fried snap rap song as he snapped it right off its case hook. He flipped up the screen to read the text. The room fell silent; the Earth stood still, his heartbeat echoed in his ears like the bass line of 90's house music. It took him a minute to realize that the only way this message zipped into his SK3's inbox was through Faye. He knew exactly what was expected of him. The memory documenting the origin of this code and his dead best friend rewound and unraveled in his head. They were joking around in Maleek's Escalade EXT and Maleek popped in the Fahrenheit 9/11 DVD. They watched and had a meaningful discussion about America's inept president George Bush and his corrupt family's dealings with kin to the most hated man of America, Osama Bin Laden. Maleek created the code out of necessity. He told Shawn that in the event that either of them ever got in a jam that their code would be their initials and 911 backwards which would signal that they needed financial assistance. It was a red alert translating to money inconspicuously finding its way to their respective wives in case they were indisposed. Shawn stared down at the text on the screen and wondered what it meant now.

"Daddy what's wrong? You look like you've seen a ghost?" Natalia waltzed into the room wrapped in a plush rose colored towel with speckles of water reflecting the early sunlight peeking in their window. Shawn shifted his focus to his half naked wife. The thought of ravaging her right then and there with the unsettling text message wrestled in his thoughts for a bit before sex tapped out rendering the "ghost message" priority number one.

"B.G., I may have to go away for a hot minute," he started to leave in search of privacy to call Faye.

"Why?" Natalia followed behind him.

"Lemme go handle something right quick and we'll talk about it when I get back okay?"

"Okay," she barely smiled as he kissed her forehead then hurried out the door.

∂∾∾§

Shawn's Escalade seemed to wink at him as he approached the gleaming heap of metal. He pressed down on his car starter remote and his ears along with passing patrons' ears were immediately overwhelmed by the blasting bass line blaring from his state of the art sub woofers.

"Shit, forgot to turn that off," he reached for his remote in the armrest caddy and turned off the elaborate system. He looked down at his Side Kick, tapped a couple of keys with his thick thumbs and started his car. He could hear the drawn out ringing in his Bluetooth headset until Faye's brash voice interrupted with.

"Hello?"

Shawn was lost in the source, enveloped by menacing scenarios. What if this was a visit from the grave? He remembered Maleek's pleas for his life, how he begged for him to let him live for Faye and the kids before he let off the fatal shot that ripped through his frontal lobe.

"I said, hello!"

"Oh, sorry about that Faye. It's Shawn. How are you?" Faye's face lit up and it was as if Shawn's voice took her to an alternate universe where her husband was still alive and joking with her "to give him the phone and stop yappin' with his man." She looked around and moved all the piles of papers and compact disks from the camel brown leather sectional and flopped down and backwards into the oversized throw pillows adorning it.

"Shawwwn! It's so good to hear your voice. It's been too long. I'm sorry about the last time we spoke. I could barely keep it together then. Sorry I didn't return your calls either. I was just trying to hold it down, you know, for the kids and all."

Shawn had attempted on many occasions before selling off his house in Atlanta and moving back to the North East to be of help to Faye but she was too distraught to accept it. Once while talking to Shawn on the phone she grilled him for leads on her husband's murderer and when he couldn't offer any useful information she slammed down the phone on him, frustrated. Shawn continued to call out of guilt but Faye never answered so he gave up and left Atlanta without saying goodbye or attending his best friend's funeral.

Faye ran a mental marathon even before Maleek's murder since her mother passed only a month earlier and she took on the responsibility of burying her mother because she was the oldest sibling. Then she was burdened with planning Maleek's funeral and shipping his body off to his mother in her native country of Montserrat. She dealt with all of this and the strain of having a multitude of bills to contend with thanks to their lavish lifestyle. Without the insurance money coming in she'd only have the measly fifty-seven grand in their bank account. That money basically belonged to all of the creditors that came out of the woodwork almost immediately after Maleek died. They made sure to have the children's college funds set up safely in educational IRAs but she avowed never to touch them because her kids were going to college even if she had to sell her ass to feed them!

"Faye, don't apologize...I know what you went—been going through. I'm just sorry for everything..." Shawn realized that his over empathizing was too much of a giveaway so he reeled his emotions back in and asked, "So that was your text I just got right?"

"Yes...um, Shawn, I'm kind of struggling financially right now. I went through Mal's things and there was a DVD with a note and it's weird but it told me to call you in case of a financial emergency."

"Yea, I figured that out. So how much and when?" he asked a bit relieved.

"Well, I wanted to just pay off Fayette and MJ's school tuition for the year, pay up the salon's mortgage for like a year then we got some other bills I want to just pay off and get it over with, you know? So, like two hundred would get me back up to speed until I can get the second salon up and running."

"I can swing that. So how do you want to do this? In increments or straight up in a duffle bag?" he, asked.

Faye, giggled and quickly blurted, "I'LL TAKE THE DUFFLE BAG ALEX!" They both laughed hysterically then after composing himself, Shawn said,

"Alright then, I'll set up and fly out there next week Wednesday. I'll meet you at the house okay?"

"Yes and thank you so much Shawn. You're such a good friend. The kids will be so happy to see you. We love you, you know that right?"

"Yea, Faye, I know and I love y'all right back. I'll call you Tuesday to remind you."

After getting off the phone with Faye Shawn felt a dull pain creeping up into his temples resting its laurels at his cranium. He knew it was only guilt consuming him. How could he ever look at his Godchildren again knowing he was the reason that they were fatherless?

ॐ

Faye's doorbell rang repeatedly and if it weren't for the fact that she was trapped behind mounds of cardboard boxes she'd have saved her ears the trauma they received from the piercing chimes.

"I'M COMING DAMMIT!" she screamed at the top of her lungs, pissed. She finally knocked down a tower of empty boxes with her swinging elbows as if she were King Kong himself maneuvering through the Big Apple. She stomped her pudgy feet to the front door and flung it open without caring to ask whom it was beforehand. When she recognized the visitor she threw her arms around the tall man's neck standing in the doorway. She squeezed with all her might while he cradled her upper body as if she were too delicate to squeeze back. She looked up into his attractive brown face and gushed.

"We missed you. Where have you been? Your cousins have been asking for you."

The man barely smiled as she backed away from him to allow him to step inside the house. He seemed troubled and Faye didn't like the fact that he wasn't his usual comedic self.

"Malcolm, what's wrong?" she asked worried. Her deceased husband's cousin looked almost exactly like him except that he was darker, a bit more slender and shorter. He bowed his head as if it were too heavy, sighed and spoke softly.

"Faye...I don't know how to tell you this shit..."

Faye gripped his forearm and asked, "What is it Malcolm?" she admired the swirling patterns of his cornrows as his bowed head began to rise. His eyes bore into hers with a sympathetic stare as he broke the shocking news he himself just heard.

"I just found out who killed Maleek," he became visibly angry and began pacing, wringing his hands, occasionally pounding his right fist into his left hand. He shook his head, gritted his teeth and exclaimed, "PB did that shit, he killed my cousin, yo...I'm gonna kill that motherfucker!" Faye's jaw dropped, her heart hurt—literally as if it were in a vise grip. She felt her knees buckle and collapsed to the floor. "No...that's not true. It can't be...Shawn loved Mal, they were like brothers, she murmured as Malcolm helped her to her feet. He guided her limp body to the sofa in the family room. He kicked one of the kid's toys out his way as he paced.

"Faye, I swear to you he will pay for this shit."

"But it can't be Shawn..."

"That's his real name? Shawn?"

"Yes."

"That's good to know. It's a wrap for that nigga!"

206

"But Shawn wouldn't...why would he kill Maleek? Why?"

Now Malcolm was conflicted. Should he give her the real answer or make up one that excluded the fact that her husband cheated on her with Shawn's wife? Should he ruin the picture perfect version of his cousin for Faye in order to preserve Maleek's memory? He decided against lying since he knew that she would find out about Maleek's bad deeds eventually. Besides, the news was out on the streets so rather than have her hear it from one of the blabber mouths at her salon he wanted to ease her into the reality of Maleek's betrayal. "Listen, what I'm about to tell you shouldn't take away from the kind of man that my cousin was. He took good care of y'all. He was a good father..."

"What the hell are you talking about?" Faye's eyes were emblazoned with sadness fused with confusion. Realizing there was no real way to cushion the blow that the truth would hit her with, Malcolm went on with giving her the bad news— straight, no chaser.

"Maleek was fucking Natalia." Her eyes widened to the size of golf balls.

"NO, NO, NOOO!" she shouted. She slumped off the sofa onto the floor and began tearing at her hair, yanking at her weave tracks as she moaned like a wounded animal. Her body shuddered with each howling sob. This was all too much information for her to handle. Malcolm hadn't a clue how to console her. He approached her cautiously for fear that she'd lash out at the messenger but she curled up on the floor and cried her eyes out instead.

"I'm so sorry, Faye...," he knelt beside her and gently rubbed her back as she trembled.

"How could he do that to me?" she muttered.

"Sometimes men can't fight temptation," Malcolm offered. Faye ignored his feeble attempt to persuade her that Maleek was somewhat a victim and then it hit her. Natalia was smiling in her face the whole time she was stabbing her in the back.

"Oooh, that backstabbing, phony, BITCH!" "I should've known that bitch was no damn good when Maleek paid me to slash some other bitch's face for her." Now Faye was really confused. The world had flipped on it's axis in the matter of minutes and the unsuspecting turn of events just kept coming. She crawled over to the sofa, pulled herself up and slouched over bracing her elbows with her knees.

"You did what?" she asked, very interested in what she was about to hear.

"Maleek hired me to mess up that model bitch Talea's face and her car over in Marietta."

"Talea! Oh, my God, Malcolm… she tried to kill herself behind that. I can't believe it…you did that?"

"Yea, Faye and I feel fucked up about that now."

"Why did Natalia want to hurt Talea?"

"Cuz she was fucking PB!"

"What the…? What's with all of this fucking around? Everybody was fucking but me! So while I was struggling with taking care of my dying mother, being stressed the fuck out of my damn mind this motherfucker was sticking his dick in my friend's pussy?!? I can't believe this shit." Faye sprang up from the sofa as if she popped right out of a toaster and paced back and forth.

"I'm saying Faye you knew that nigga wasn't trying to fuck up what y'all had so I know that she must've thrown the pussy at him. Mal wasn't trying to catch no heat from you for another bitch."

Faye ignored Malcolm's bullshit excuse for her dead, cheating husband and came out of left field with.

"I want those lying, phony motherfuckers to hurt just like me and my babies. Will you help me?"

"Whatever you need I got you. How do you want to handle this?"

"First things first, that murdering bastard P.B. is

supposed to bring me some money so we need to set his ass up. I want to be there, for him to see me before y'all fuck his ass up. He sat up there and cried to me like he really gave a fuck about Mal, me and the kids! I wanna shoot this nigga dick off!"

"Damn, y'all women don't play," Malcolm chuckled and shook his head then said, "But I can arrange that. Now, what about his wifey?"

"Oh, that bitch is mine. I'll take care of her ass. You just make sure that they don't kill PB. I have plans for his ass. They're gonna suffer."

BEAT
THE
CROSS

A Thriller By
LEON BLUE

CHAPTER 1

Rico Adams was expecting a call that would either make him wealthy or get a lot of people killed, maybe both. He was at the car wash vacuuming his brother's Lexus LS 400 when he heard a vehicle pick up speed. The driver was coming for him. He caught a glimpse of the approaching car and wasted no time jumping up on the concrete base of the vacuum cleaner.

The driver slammed on brakes, threw the car in park, and got out laughing. "Get your mutha fuckin scared ass down."

"What in the...fuck..." Rico stepped down from the cemented vacuum base and kicked the hose as hard as he could. "Trex, that stupid shit is funny to you? You gonna make me fuck your momma's son up." Their attention shifted to the police car that cruised by. The cop glanced at the two black males but kept going.

"How long you got the Lexus?" Trexler Orson looked inside the back window of the car.

"Fuck the Lexus. Don't your black ass get tired of playing?"

"Playing? I don't even play the muthafuckin radio. I was tryin' to kill you for real."

Rico's pager sounded off. He checked the display then walked to the driver's door of the Lexus, leaned inside, and dialed the number using the car phone.

"Computer 411, Dave speaking."

"What's up, Dave? Why didn't you put in your code? I almost didn't call your ass back."

"How fast can you get here?"

"Ten minutes."

"Did you find a good thief with balls?"

"Yep."

"Bring him if you can, but remember the game plan. And not a word about the casino."

"I'm on my way." Rico terminated the call. He pulled himself out of the door way of the car and smiled at Trexler.

"Drive to my house and park. Dave, at the computer shop, is waiting for us."

"The white guy? And I thought you was lying about having that connection." Trex rubbed the tips of his fingers with both thumbs. The marred, gritty feel was fresh. "You got your finger prints straight?"

"They're coming back now. I'll clip them again when I get to the house."

"Wait a minute." Trex rushed to his Camry and retrieved the fingernail clippers from the console. He pitched them to Rico. "I stole them from your house last night."

"I don't know why; you didn't have a job to pull off."

"It's a business world...stay out of mine." Trex got in the Camry and drove away.

Rico was driving down Heckle Boulevard when the car phone rang. He answered it by pressing the button on the steering wheel. "Tank is at work, and can I take a message?"

"Dad, I ain't looking for Tank; I'm looking for you."

Rico lowered the volume on the intercom. "Roc, why do you talk so damn loud?"

"Shit, I don't know. My momma say I take after you."

"What's up? I'll be there in a few minutes."

"Two of your girlfriends called here at the same time."

"Same time? You sound like they was together."

"No, I clicked over and Sequerria was on the other line."

"You didn't mix the damn names up, did you?"

"Hell no. You know I got your back, Dad."

Rico laughed. He thought about how fast his son was growing up. The boy was already passing to the ninth grade.

"Did your momma call you today?"

"Yeah. She asked me if I was ready to come home."

"What did you tell her?"

"I told her that school only been out a week. She knew I was staying the whole summer."

"You told her I was gone?

"No, because she think I'm too young to be here by myself. She wanted to speak to you, but I told her you was outside arguing with one of your girl friends. She started laughing."

"Boy, you're the smartest little fucka on the planet."

"Then stop by the store and get me some Doritos."

"You got that." Rico terminated the call and smiled.

DAVE CLOSED THE BLINDS and displayed the 'closed' sign in the all¬glass front door. He heard someone knocking at the back door of his shop. On the way to the back, he stepped inside his office and pressed the button on the smoke detector. The chirp was sharp, and he knew the recording would be just as clear. He heard knocking at the door.

Dave made it to the back door and saw Rico through the peephole. He unlocked the door and invited him in. Rico was closely followed by Trex.

"Wait a second. Who's your company?" Dave attempted to keep Trex at bay with an open¬hand gesture. Trex stared at the hand and walked around it.

"That's my business partner. I have no business without my partner."

"But I asked you to come alone. This is—"

"You're just wasting good time. I trust my man here more than I trust you."

"Well, I have a business partner, too, but I didn't want you to feel uncomfortable with his presence."

"If it's any consolation, I make my own comfort by bringing along my own partner."

Trex walked closer to Dave. "Call your partner; we'll wait for him. Otherwise let's shorten the language arts and get to the purpose of this visit."

Dave turned away, avoiding the menacing stare. "Let's go to my office."

Rico and Trex sat on the leather sofa and watched Dave on the other side of the desk. Dave looked at Rico.

"Are you familiar with Novelty Bread?" he asked.

"Everybody in Rock Hill is familiar with Novelty," Trex leaned forward.

"The question wasn't directed at you." Dave feigned a smile.

Trex leaned back and stared at the painting above the file cabinet.

"Yeah, what about the bread store?" Rico made eye contact with Dave.

"There's two van-like trucks parked in the back of the store; I want you to steal them between 5:10 and 5:20 on Monday morning."

"You want me to steal some silly-¬ass trucks—"

"Don't concern your—"

Rico got up from the sofa and Trex followed suit. "I don't steal cars and trucks. Ain't enough money in that shit."

Dave opened his desk drawer, but before he could remove the contents, Trex had drawn a .45 caliber handgun.

"Take your hand out of the drawer, slowly, or I'll lower your muthafuckin blood pressure."

Dave eased his hand out gripping a band of hundred¬dollar bills.

Rico calmly pushed Trex's extended arm away then took a seat again.

Trex remained standing, anxious.

Dave dropped the money on the desk.

"You'll make five grand just for stealing two trucks. Half the money is up front right now. The other half when you get the trucks to the desired location and–"
The telephone rang.

"You mind?" Dave looked at Rico.

"Answer it; it's your phone," answered Rico.

"Computer 411, Dave speaking."

"I'm on my way to the shop. Did the Rico guy show up? I have the ID ready."

"Yeah, Mark. You just interrupted our meeting. I'll see you when you get here." Dave replaced the receiver.

"Five grand for some bread trucks." Trex tucked the gun away. "Sounds like there's some risky shit you ain't telling us about."

"Could you shut your partner's mouth before he blows this deal for you?" Dave frowned at Rico.

Trex inhaled deeply and released.

Rico looked down at the floor, scratching his head. *What the fuck was my next line?* He flinched at the sound of the .45 and looked up, surprised.

Trex jumped up on the desk and squatted, looking at Dave's bleeding shoulder. "Blow the deal? We takin' the twenty-five hundred and everything else you got in this muthafucka."

Rico shook his head in disbelief. He heard the sound of the .45 again.

ORDER FORM

TERI WOODS PUBLISHING
P.O. BOX 20069
NEW YORK, NY 10001
(201) 840-8660
WWW.TERIWOODSPUBLISHING.COM

PURCHASER INFORMATION:

NAME _____

ADDRESS_____

_____

CITY_____ STATE____ ZIP_____

PURCHASING INFORMATION:
(Please mark the books you are ordering)

TRUE TO THE GAME I   _____
TRUE TO THE GAME II   _____
TRUE TO THE GAME III   _____
B-MORE CAREFUL   _____
THE ADVENTURES GHETTO SAM   _____
DUTCH I   _____
DUTCH II   _____
TELL ME YOUR NAME   _____
TRIANGLE OF SINS   _____
RECTANGLE OF SINS   _____
DEADLY REIGNS I   _____
DEADLY REIGNS II   _____
DEADLY REIGNS III   _____
ANGEL   _____
DOUBLE DOSE   _____
PREDATORS   _____
ALIBI   _____
BEAT THE CROSS   _____

PRICING INFORMATION:
Book Cost $14.95
Shipping/Handling $ 4.05
Total $19.00

INMATE PRICING INFORMATION
(For Order being shipped to inmates only)
Book Cost $11.21
Shipping/Handling $ 4.05
Total $15.26

MANUSCRIPT SUBMISSION GUIDELINES

TERI WOODS PUBLISHING
P.O. BOX 20069
NEW YORK, NY 10001
(201) 840-8660
WWW.TERIWOODSPUBLISHING.COM

Teri Woods Publishing accepts solicited and unsolicited manuscripts. We do not, however, accept short stories, poetry or screenplays. We ask that manuscripts be forwarded in their entirety along with a brief synopsis and a cover letter. Your manuscript must be a minimum of 70,000 words, typed, double-spaced, on regular 8½" by 11" paper. You <u>must</u> send in a self addressed stamped envelope at the time of your submission should your manuscript be rejected and you wish for it to be sent back to you. All manuscripts received will be *discarded* once they are rejected if they are not sent in with a self-addressed, stamped envelope.

Once your manuscript is received, it will be cataloged by the postmark date and you will receive a letter of acknowledgement. Please note, it generally takes three to six months for a manuscript to be reviewed, however it can take longer. Please do not call inquiring about your manuscript status. When the review process is completed you will be notified.

Thank you for inquiring with Teri Woods Publishing, the largest independent publisher in the country.